I0615327

Frederick Victor Dickins

The Old Bamboo-Hewer's Story - (Taketori no ikina no monogatari)

The Earliest of the Japanese Romances, Written in the Tenth Century

Frederick Victor Dickins

The Old Bamboo-Hewer's Story - (Taketori no ikina no monogatari)
The Earliest of the Japanese Romances, Written in the Tenth Century

ISBN/EAN: 9783337050337

Printed in Europe, USA, Canada, Australia, Japan

Cover: Foto ©Andreas Hilbeck / pixelio.de

More available books at **www.hansebooks.com**

THE OLD BAMBOO-HEWER'S STORY

(TAKETORI NO OKINA NO MONOGATARI).

THE EARLIEST OF THE JAPANESE ROMANCES,

WRITTEN IN THE TENTH CENTURY.

TRANSLATED, WITH OBSERVATIONS AND NOTES,

BY

F. VICTOR DICKINS.

WITH THREE CHROMO-LITHOGRAPHIC ILLUSTRATIONS TAKEN
FROM JAPANESE MAKIMONO.

TO WHICH IS ADDED THE ORIGINAL TEXT IN ROMAN, WITH
GRAMMAR, ANALYTICAL NOTES, AND VOCABULARY.

LONDON:
TRÜBNER & CO., LUDGATE HILL.

1888.

ILLUSTRATIONS.

TO FACE PAGE

THE OREAD'S* HAUNT 12

THE UPBEARING OF THE LADY KAGUYA 32

FUJISAN FROM THE PASS OF GOKANYA 36

* Erroneously lettered The Dreads' Haunt.

ERRATA.

By an oversight a conjecture of Daishu's is given on p. 9
as the translation of the last two lines of the ode;
the version should be: "O that heedless of yonder
bowl (by the word-play, 'of the shame of my ill-
success') the Lady might still listen to my suit!"

On p. 19 the last two lines of the ode should be rendered,
"O, would I have exposed it to so unexpected a
fate!"—by the word-play, "far from the fierce flame
kept would I have feasted my eyes upon it!"

THE STORY OF THE OLD BAMBOO-HEWER.

(TAKETORI NO OKINA NO MONOGATARI.)

A JAPANESE ROMANCE OF THE TENTH CENTURY.

THE COMING OF THE LADY KAGUYA AND THE DAYS OF
CHILDHOOD.

(KAGUYA HIME NO OITACHI.)

FORMERLY [1] there lived an old man, a bamboo-hewer, who
hewed bamboos on the bosky hill-side, and manywise he
wrought them to serve men's needs, and his name was
Sanugi no Miyakko.[2] Now one day, while plying the
hatchet in a grove of bamboos, was he suddenly ware of a
tall stem, whence streamed forth through the gloom a dazzling
light. Much marvelling, he drew nigh to the reed, and saw
that the glory proceeded from the heart thereof, and he
looked again and beheld a tiny creature, a palm's breadth
in stature and of rare loveliness, which stood midmost the
splendour. Then he said to himself, " Day after day, from
dawn to dusk, toil I among these bamboo-reeds, and this
child that abides amidst them I may surely claim as mine
own." So he put forth his hand, and took the tiny being,
and carried it home, and gave it to the goodwife and her

---

[1] *Mukashi*—here, as often, equivalent to the Latin ' olim.'
[2] Or Saruki, or Sadaki. Sanugi, or Sanuki, is a province of Shikoku.
Miyakko is *miya-tsu-ko*, servant of the August Home, that is, of the Court or
Palace, equivalent to *ason* (*a-omi, asobi*) or Baron. The expression was also
used in the sense of 'ruler,' 'governor.' But, like many other titles, it degenerated,
as here, into a mere name.

women to be nourished. And passing fair was the child, but so frail and tender that it was needful to place it in a basket to be reared. But after lighting upon this gift whilst hewing bamboos, he ceased not from his daily toil, and night after night, as he shore through the reeds and opened their internodes, came he upon one filled with grain of gold, and so, ere long, he amassed great wealth. Meanwhile the child, being duly tended, grew daily in stature, and after three months—wonderful to relate!—her stature was as that of a maiden of full years. Then her tresses were lifted [1] and she donned the robe of maidenhood, but still came not forth from behind the curtain.[2] Thus cherished and watched over and tenderly reared, grew she fair of form, nor could the world show her like, and there was no gloom in any corner of the dwelling, but brightness reigned throughout, nor ever did the Ancient fall into a sorrowful mood but that his sadness was chased away when he beheld the maiden, nor was any angry word ever heard beneath that roof, and happily the days went by. Long the Ancient hewed bamboos, and gathered gold, and thus it was that he came to flourish exceedingly in the land. After this wise grew the girl to maidenhood, and the Ancient named her Mimurodo Imube no Akita, but she was more commonly called the Lady Kaguya, the Precious Slender Bamboo of the Field of Autumn.[3] Then for three days a great feast was held, and

---

[1] Anciently the hair was allowed to fall in long tresses on either shoulder. At the age of 13 or 14 these were brought up and fastened in a sort of knot on the crown or side of the head. The custom is alluded to in a "tanka" of the Manyōshu (The Myriad Leaves—an Anthology of the tenth century):

Tachibana no	Under the long-roof bright with the hues reflected
tereru nagaya ni	from the orange-blooms,
waga ineshi:	have I slumbered—
unahi bakari wa	a girl of tender years,
kami agetsuran ka?	shall my tresses ever be bound up?

[2] Hung before the *toko*, or alcove, or upper end of the house-place. The meaning is that she remained within her mother's care, unbetrothed and unmarried.

[3] *Mimurodo* means the place of three caves, alluding, perhaps, to the aboriginal habit (still practised in Yezo) of living in caves or half-underground huts. It is sometimes written *mimoro*, which has the signification of a sacred (*mi*) place. *Imube* (*imbe* or *imibe*) were originally the hereditary builders of Shinto shrines. In certain provinces—Sanuki was one—the designation became a family-name. Mr. Satow explains it as signifying an association (*me* or *be*) eschewing (*imi*) uncleanness. *Akita* is the Field of Autumn, more strictly the laboured field made

the neighbours, one and all, menfolk and womenfolk, were invited, and they came in merry crowds and noble was the revelry.[1]

THE WOOING OF THE MAIDEN.
(TSUMA-GOI.)

Now the gentles dwelling in those parts, men of name and eke men of low degree, thought of nothing but how they might win this fair maiden to wife, or even gaze upon her beauty, and so distracted were they with love that they let their passion be plain to all the world.[2] Around the fence and about the porch they lingered, but in vain, for no glimpse of the maiden could be got, nor slept they when night came but wandered out in the darkness, and made holes here and there in the fence and peered through these, but to no purpose did they strain their eyes, for never caught they sight of her on whom they longed to gaze, and thus sped their wooing from the twilight-hour of the monkey onwards. Well-nigh beside themselves were they with love and woe, but no sign was vouchsafed them, and though they essayed to gain speech of some among the household, no word of answer ever got they. So it was, yet many a noble suitor still lingered thereabouts, watching through the livelong day and through the livelong night, to catch some glimpse of the

---

ready in late autumn for the rice-sowing. It is a not uncommon place-name. The whole subject of Japanese place, family, and personal names awaits investigation. *Kaguya* is often written 赤赤 映 'illumer of darkness,' hence, perhaps, the present legend. On the other hand, it may, and probably did originally, mean simply the Princess or Goddess (*hi me*, i.e. glorious lady) of Kaguyama, or Kago-yama (deer-hill, as Kagoshima is deer-island), the *ya* being an emphatic suffix. Kaguyama is the subject of an oft-quoted stanza, said to have been composed by the Emperor Jitō (A.D. 690–696) on beholding the mountain bathed in a flood of summer sunlight (some say moonlight):

Haru sugite	The spring hath passed away,
natsu ki ni kerashi :	and the summer hath come ;
shiro tayo no	and the pure white raiment (of the gods)
koromo hosu chō	is spread out belike,
Ama no Kaguyama !	on the slopes of Amonokagu !

[1] Such appears to be the meaning of the text, here probably corrupt. The original is *otoko ōna kirawazu yobitsudoyete īto kushikoku asobu*, which the commentary thus explains, *otoko onna no kirai naku nigiwashiku yobitsudoyetaru nari*. Another reading is *otoko wa ukekirawazu yo hi hodoyete*, etc.

[2] Which was contrary to good manners, and so a proof of the intensity of their love.

maiden; but those of low degree after a time bethought them
'twere vain to pace up and down thus bootlessly, and they
departed and came no more. But there tarried five suitors,
true lovers, and worthier of the name belike, in whose hearts,
love died not down, and night and day they still haunted the
spot. And these noble lovers were the Prince Ishizukuri[1]
and the Prince Kuramochi, the Sadaijin Dainagon Abe no
Miushi and the Chiunagon Ōtomo no Miyuki, and Morotada,
the Lord of Iso.

When a woman is somewhat fairer than the crowd of
women, how greatly do men long to gaze upon her beauty!
How much more filled with desire to behold the rare loveliness of the Lady Kaguya were these lords, who would touch
no food, nor could wean their thoughts from her, and continued to pace up and down without the fence, albeit their
pain was thus in no wise eased. They indited supplications,
but no answer was vouchsafed; they offered stanzas of com-
plaint, but these too were disregarded; yet their love lessened
no whit, and they affronted the ice and snow of winter and
the thunderous heats of mid-summer[2] with equal fortitude.
So passed the days, and upon a certain day these lords
summoned the Hewer and prayed him to bestow his daughter
upon one of them, bowing before him and rubbing their
palms together suppliantwise. But he said: "No child of
mine by blood is the maiden, nor can she be constrained
to follow my will." And the days and the months went by,
and the lords returned to their mansions, but their thoughts
still dwelt upon the Maiden, and many a piteous prayer they
made, and many a supplication they indited, nor cared they
to cease their wooing, for surely, they said to themselves,
the Maiden might not remain unmated for ever. And they

---

[1] These names, at least such as require it, will be explained below.

[2] *Minazuki*, i.e. *Kami-nashi-tsuki*, part of July and August under the old
calendar. The name signifies "godless month," because during it all the gods
were believed to be absent from the world holding council in the bed of the Stream of
Heaven (the Milky Way), to determine the fortunes of men during the ensuing
year. This legend is of Chinese origin, as indeed are most Japanese legends in a
greater or less degree, and embodies, perhaps, some memory of the time when the
ancestors of the Chinese dwelt about the sources of the Yellow River, which was
supposed to be the continuation on earth of the Stream of Heaven.

continued their suit, and so plainly did they manifest the strength of their passion that the Ancient was constrained to say to the Maiden, "By the grace of Buddha,[1] through the cycle of changes hast thou come to us, daughter, and from babe to maid have we cherished thee, and I pray thee hearken to the words of an old man who loveth thee passing well."

And the Maiden answered:

"What might my father say that his daughter would not give dutiful ear to? I know not if I came to thee through the cycle of changes, but this I know, that thou art my dear father."

Then the Ancient replied:

"Right happy do thy words make me, daughter; but consider, I am an old man whose years outnumber seventy, to-day I may pass away or to-morrow, and 'tis the way of the world that the youth cleave to the maid, and the maid to the youth, for thus the world increaseth, nor otherwise are things ordered."

But Kaguya said:

"Oh father, what mean these words you utter; must it then be as you say?"

"Ay," replied the Ancient, "though strangely hast thou come to us through the cycle of changes, yet hast thou the nature of a woman, while such are thy father's years that he may not long tarry in the world to protect thee. These lords have sought thee to wife for months and years, listen, prithee, to their supplication, and let them have speech with thee, each in due turn."

Kaguya answered:

"Not so fair am I that I may be certain of a man's faith, and were I to mate with one whose heart proved fickle, what a miserable fate were mine! Noble lords, without doubt, are these of whom thou speakest, but I would not wed a man whose heart should be all untried and unknown."

---

[1] Or "my child, my Buddha," *i.e.* "my darling."

And the Ancient said :

"Thou speakest my very thoughts, daughter. But, prithee, what manner of man hast thou a mind to mate with? Assuredly these lords are of noble nature and nurture."

Then she answered :

"Nay, 'tis but that that I would know what the quality of these noble gentlemen's constancy may be. So like are the hearts of men that one may by no means easily part the better from the worse; go, I pray you, to these lords, and say to them, your daughter will follow him who shall prove himself the worthiest to mate with."

And the Ancient, nodding assent to her words, said :

"'Tis well."

Now the night fell, and the suitors assembled and serenaded the Maiden with flute-music and with singing, with chanting to accompaniments and piping, and with cadenced tap and clap of fan, in the midst whereof came forth the Ancient, and thus spake them :

"Months and years have my lords tarried by this poor hut, and their servant presents his respectful homage and ventures to offer his humble gratitude for their high favour. But many are his years, and he knows not whether he may pass away to-day or to-morrow. After this wise hath he spoken to the Maiden and prayed her to choose one among your lordships for a husband; but she would fain learn which of you be the worthiest, and him alone will she wed. Fair seemed her speech to your servant, perchance your lordships, too, will not disdain her words." And they nodded assent, saying: "It is well." Whereupon the Ancient went within and spoke with the damsel, and thus she expressed her will :

"In Tenjiku¹ is a beggar's bowl of stone, which, of old, the Buddha himself bore, in quest whereof let Prince Ishizukuri depart and bring me the same. And on the mountain

¹ The Japanese form of the Chinese Buddhist name for Northern India, said to be a corruption of "Shiutuh," or the Chinese form of the name now known as Sciude.

Hôrai, that towers over the Eastern ocean, grows a tree with roots of silver and trunk of gold and fruitage of pure white jade, and I bid Prince Kuramochi fare thither and break off and bring me a branch thereof. Again in the land of Moro-koshi men fashion fur-robes of the pelt of the Flame-proof Rat, and I pray the Dainagon to find me one such. Then of the Chiunagon I require the rainbow-hued jewel that hides its sparkle deep in the dragon's head; and from the hands of the Lord of Iso would I fain receive the cowry-shell that the swallow brings hither over the broad sea-plain."

But the Ancient said:

"Terrible tasks these be—the things thou requirest, daughter, are not to be found within the four seas; how may one bid these noble lords depart upon like quests?"

"Nay," quoth the damsel, "these be no tasks beyond stout men's strength."

Thereupon the Ancient saw that there was nothing for it but to obey, and he went out from her, and told the suitors all that had passed, saying:

"Thus hath it been willed, and these are the tasks that must be accomplished that your worth may be known."

But the princes and the lords murmured among them-selves, and said:

"'Tis, forsooth, that the Lady holds in disdain our courteous suit." So they turned and with heavy hearts fared each to his own home.

THE SACRED BEGGING-BOWL OF THE BUDDHA.

(HOTOKE NO MI ISHI NO HACHI.)

Now the days to come seemed void of pleasure to Prince Ishizukuri [1] if never he might gaze upon the Lady's beauty, and he fell to turning over in his mind whether he might not light upon the Holy Buddha's bowl if he went up and down the

---

[1] *Ishizukuri no miko. Miko* is noble (*mi*) child (*ko*), originally a prince of the blood royal. *Ishizukuri (tsukuri)* may mean 'stone-built,' or, in a bad sense, 'stone-counterfeit.' *Sei-yô zukuri* is still a common expression for 'western-fashioned.'

land of Tenjiku in search thereof.   But the Prince cared not
to set out lightly on such a journey, and after much pondering over the matter he bethought himself it were after all a
vain quest to fare tens of thousands of leagues on the chance
of finding, in all the broad land of Tenjiku, a certain
beggar's dish.   Therefore, he let it be made known to the
Lady that he had that very day undertaken the Quest; but
towards Tenjiku he fared not a league, but hid him in
Yamato, and abode there three years, at the end whereof, in
a hill-monastery in Tōchi, he found upon an altar of Binzuru[1]
a bowl blackened by age and begrimed with smoke, which
he took and wrapped in a web of brocade.   He then attached
the gift to an artificial Bloom-branch,[2] and sought again the
dwelling of the Lady Kaguya, and caused the gift to be
carried in to her.   And as she looked upon the Bowl she
marvelled greatly, and in it lay a scroll, which she opened,
and a stanza was writ thereon :

Umi yama no	Over seas, over hills
michi no kokoro wo	hath thy servant fared, and weary
tsukushi-hate :	and wayworn he perisheth :
ishi no hachi no	O what tears hath cost this bowl of stone,
namida nagare wa ![3]	what floods of streaming tears !

Then the Lady looked again to see if the Bowl shone with
light,[4] but not so much as a firefly's twinkle could she
discover, and she caused the bowl to be returned to the
Prince, and with it was bestowed a scroll whereon was writ
a verse :

---

[1] Pindola, the Succourer in Sickness, one of the sixteen Rakan. In the *Butsu-zō-zui* this Arhat (Rakan) is the first enumerated, and is called Hatsura tasha. He is represented as an old man seated by the edge of a precipice overlooking the sea, and holding in his right hand a feather-brush (?) to keep off flies, in his left a scroll (or tablet ?) of the law.

[2] It was a pretty custom in Old Japan to accompany a gift with a branch of peach or plum or wild cherry in full bloom.

[3] The last two lines, by a word-play, may be read *ishi no wa chi no namida nagare wa ?* which would mean 'of a truth this stone hath been the bed of a stream of tears of blood.' In winter, when the rivers in Japan are at their driest, the stony central portion of the broad river-bed is laid bare, along which flows the diminished stream.

[4] The intrinsic splendour of a true relic of the Buddha is meant.

Oku tsuyu no	Of the hanging dewdrop
hikari wo da ni mo	not even the passing sheen
yadosumashi :	dwells herein :
Ogura yama nite	On the Hill of Darkness, the Hill of Ogura,[1]
nani motomekemu?	what couldest thou hope to find ?

Thereupon the Prince cast away the Bowl and made answer thuswise :

Shirayama[2] ni	Nay, on the Hill of Brightness
ayeba hikari no	what splendour
usuru ka to :	will not pale ?
hachi wo sutete mo	would that away from the light of thy beauty
tanomaruru kana !	the sheen of yonder Bowl might prove me true !

But no answer would the Lady make, nor give ear to any supplication, and the Prince, wearied with bootless complainings, after awhile turned him sadly away and departed. And still men say of a crestfallen fellow, "hachi (haji) wo suteru."[3]

---

[1] Situate in the district in which the Bowl had been found. In *gura* (*kura* with *nigori*) is involved the sense of darkness *(kurashi)*, though the character used in writing the name means "granary." So in a *tanka* (ode) of the Manyōshu :—

Yuu sareba,	As the shades of evening fall
Ogura no yama ni	on the Hill of Ogura,
naku shika no	the calling deer
koyoi wa nakazu,	cease this night their cry,
ine ni kerashi !	and in slumber is wrapped the world.

And again :—

Ohoigawa	On the waters of the Ohoi
ukayeru fune no	float the fisher-barks ;
kagari-bi ni	was it in the glare of their decoy-fires,
Ogura no yama wa	O Hill of Ogura,
na nomi narikeri !	thou gainedst thy name ?

[2] Shirayama is said to be opposite in situation as in the meaning involved in its name (originally, no doubt, *Shiroyama* or Castle Hill, but corrupted into *Shirayama* or White Hill), to Ogurayama. The intrinsic brilliance of the Bowl was lost in that of the Lady's beauty, if it were cast aside out of her presence its sheen would become visible.

[3] *Hachi*, bowl, by *nigori* becomes *haji*, shame ; hence the word-play, conveying a sense of the shame which attends the defeat of a tricky and dishonest scheme.

The Jewel-Bearing Branch of Mount Hōrai.
(Hōrai no tama no yeda.)

Of a wily turn was Prince Kuramochi, and he gave out to
the world that he was about to take the baths in the land of
Tsukushi, but to the Lady Kaguya he let it be declared that
he was setting out upon the Quest after the Jewel-laden
Branch.   So he fared towards Naniwa with some of his
squires, but not many, for he alleged him fain to travel
without state, and took with him but a few of those who
were in closest attendance upon their lord, and even these,
after they had watched him with their eyes as he took boat,
went back to Miako.   Thus the Prince made folk think he
had departed faring towards Tsukushi or towards Hōrai, but
he tarried three days at Naniwa, and then turned him again
capitalwards, being sculled up-stream.   Beforehand all needful commands had been given, and six men of the Uchimaro
family, the most noted craftsmen of the time, had been
sought out and lodged in a dwelling aloof from the world-
ways and surrounded with a triple fence, and there the
Prince too retreated.   Then he furnished the chief of the
craftsmen with resources drawn from sixteen of his farms,[1]
the produce of which he allotted to that purpose, and caused
furnaces to be erected and a jewel-laden branch to be
fashioned differing no whit from that which the Lady
Kaguya had bidden him go in quest of.   Thus cunningly
the Prince laid his scheme, and taking the branch with him
set off secretly, and embarking in a boat journeyed down to
Naniwa, whence he let it be made known to his squires that
he had returned, and assuming the guise of one terribly
worn and spent with travel, awaited their coming.   And his
squires and retainers came accordingly to meet him, where-

---

[1] This seems to be the general sense of an obscure and probably corrupt
passage—*shirasetamattaru kagiri jiuroku so woo* (o?) *kami ni kudo wo akete*, etc.
I have followed the hints given in the commentary of Ohide.   Perhaps the passage
ought to read, *jiuroku sho* (so) *no kami no kura*, etc.   Another commentator suggests
that *So o kami* is the county of Sōkami, and retains *kudo*, furnace, the reference
then being to sixteen furnaces or pottery ovens in Sōkami.   But this interpretation seems far-fetched.   Possibly a sort of pun is intended on the Prince's name,
Kuramochi, which really meaning (*Kuruma-mochi*), " guardian or keeper of the
Mikado's carriages," may also be read as signifying " superintendent of the
Royal treasuries or granaries."

upon the Prince caused the Branch to be placed in a coffer which was covered with brocade, and a clamour arose as he went through the city. "Wonderful! the Prince Kuramochi comes up to the capital, bearing with him the Udonge[1] in bloom." But the Lady Kaguya, when these tidings reached her, said to herself, "This Prince hath surely gotten the better of me," and her heart broke within her. While thus matters stood was heard a knocking at the entrance, and presently it was announced that the Prince had presented himself and begged to be permitted to speak with the Lady, although still wearing his travelling-garb, for he had perilled his life in the quest after the Jewel-laden Branch, and had won it, and now desired to lay it at her feet. The Ancient received the message, and took the Branch and carried it within, and attached to it was a scroll whereon was written a stanza :

Itazura ni,   Though it were at the peril

 mi wa nashitsu tomo, of my very life,

  tama no yo wo without the Jewel-laden Branch

taorade, saye wa   in my hands never again

kayerazaramashi ! would I have dared to return !

But the Lady looked on the Branch and was sad, and the Ancient came to her hastily, saying, "'Tis the very branch, daughter, thou desiredst the Prince to bring thee from Mount Hōrai, and he has accomplished the Quest thou badest him undertake without failing in any particular, nor mayst thou delay his guerdon ; without tarrying to change his raiment, and before seeking his own mansion, has he hasted hither, nor longer canst thou refuse his suit."

But the maiden answered nothing, resting her chin mournfully on her palm, while the tears streamed in floods over her cheeks. Meanwhile the Prince, thinking that now he need dread no denial, remained waiting in the porch-way, and the Ancient resuming, said : "The like of this Jewel-laden Branch is not to be found within the four seas, thou

---

[1] The Buddhist Udumbara ; the fig-tree (*Ficus glomerata*), believed to flower once only in three thousand years, hence the expression is used in respect of anything very rare and marvellous.

canst not refuse the promised guerdon, nor is the Prince un-
comely of person."

But the Lady answered: "Hard it is thus still to oppose
my father's will, but this thing is deemed unattainable
whereof I laid the quest upon the Prince, yet how easily
hath he won it; a bitter grief it is to thy daughter." Then
the Ancient fell to busying himself with putting the chamber
in order, and after awhile went out and accosted the Prince
again, saying: "Your servant would fain know what manner
of place it may be where grows this tree—how wonderful a
thing it is, and lovely and pleasant to see!" And the Prince
answered: "The year before yesteryear, on the tenth of the
second month (*Kisaragi*), we took boat at Naniwa and sculled
out into the ocean, not knowing what track to follow; but I
thought to myself, what would be the profit of continuing
life if I might not attain the desire of my heart; so pressed
we onwards, blown where the wind listed. If we perished
even what mattered it, while we lived we would make what
way we could over the sea-plain, and perchance thus might
we somehow reach the mountain men do call Hōrai. So re-
solved we sculled further and further over the heaving
waters, until far behind us lay the shores of our own land.
And as we wandered thus, now deep in the trough of the sea
we saw its very bottom, now blown by the gale we came to
strange lands, where creatures like demons fell upon us
and were like to have slain us Now, knowing neither
whence we had come nor whither we tended, we were almost
swallowed up by the sea ; now, failing of food we were
driven to live upon roots; now, again, indescribably terrible
beings came forth and would have devoured us; or we had
to sustain our bodies by eating of the spoil of the sea.
Beneath strange skies were we, and no human creature was
there to give us succour; to many diseases fell we prey as we
drifted along knowing not whitherwards, and so tossed we
over the sea-plain, letting our boat follow the wind for five
hundred days. Then, about the hour of the dragon, four
hours ere noon, saw we a high hill looming faintly over the
watery waste. Long we gazed at it, and marvelled at the

majesty of the mountain rising out of the sea. Lofty it was
and fair of form, and doubting not it was the mountain
we were seeking, our hearts were filled with awe. We plied
the oar, and coasted it for two days or three, and then we
saw a woman, arrayed like an angel, come forth out of the
hills, bearing a silver vessel which she filled with water.
So we landed and accosted her, saying : 'How call men this
mountain?' and she said, ''Tis Mount Hōrai,' whereat our
hearts were filled with joy. 'And you, who tell us this, who
then are you,' we inquired. 'My name is Hōkanruri,' she
answered, and thereupon suddenly withdrew among the hills.
On scanning the mountain, we saw no man could climb its
slopes, so steep were they, and we wandered about the foot
thereof, where grew trees bearing blooms the world cannot show
the like of. There we found a stream flowing down from the
mountain, the waters whereof were rainbow-hued, yellow as
gold, white as silver, blue as precious ruri ;[1] and the stream
was spanned by bridges built up of divers gems, and by it
grew trees laden with dazzling jewels, and from one of these
I broke off the branch which I venture now to offer to the
Lady Kaguya. An evil deed, I fear me, but how could
I do otherwise than accomplish the object of my Quest?
Delightful beyond all words is yonder mountain, in all the
world there exists not its like. After I had plucked off the
branch, my heart brake within me, and I hasted on board,
and we sped hitherwards with a fair wind behind us, and
after some four hundred days came to Naniwa, whence
I departed without tarrying, so great was my desire to lay
the Branch at the feet of the Lady, nor did I even change my
raiment, soddened with the brine of ocean."

Moved by the piteous tale the Ancient composed a stanza :

Kuretake no	Amid the gloomy bamboo-groves
yoyo no take toru	long long have I hewed bamboos,
noyama ni mo :	even upon the wild hill-sides ;
saya wa wabishiki	but thus sad an internode
fushi wo nomi miji !	(thus sad a fortune) never have
	I beheld.

[1] See below.

The Prince read the verse and said: " For these many days have I endured misery, now methinks shall I know peace," and indited a stanza in reply :

Waga tamoto	The sleeve of my garment
kiyo kawakereba,	but this day hath become dry,
wabishiki no	and of miseries
chigusa [1] no kazu mo	the countless kinds I have endured
wasurarenubeshi !	no longer will be remembered by me.

At this juncture came six men within the fence, one after the other, and one of them carried a cleft bamboo, bearing a scroll in the cleft, and said: "The chief of the craftsmen, Ayabe no Uchimaro, humbly represents that he and his fellows for the space of a thousand days broke their hearts and spent their strength in fashioning the Jewel-laden Branch. Yet, though long and heavy their labours, they have received no wage for their toil, and he humbly prays that they may be accorded due payment that they may have wherewithal to buy food for their wives and little ones." Then he lifted up the bamboo with the scroll in its cleft. The Ancient, with his head on one side, marvelled as he heard the words of the craftsman, but the Prince was beside himself with dismay, and felt his liver perish within him. And the Lady Kaguya, hearing of the matter, commanded that the scroll should be brought to her, whereupon it was taken within and unrolled and thus was it writ thereon : "Lately His Highness shut himself up with us mean craftsmen, and caused a jewel-laden branch of the rarest beauty to be fashioned, and promised me by way of guerdon the mastership of the craft. And after pondering over the matter, coming to know that the Branch was to be bestowed upon the Lady Kaguya, who was about to become a Lady of the Palace, I deemed it well to seek aid at the Lady's dwelling that my guerdon might be given me and the wages due be paid to us."

---

[1] *Chigusa*, thousand herbs—an expression signifying a thousand kinds, or the innumerable, that is, all kinds and varieties of wretchedness.

As the Lady Kaguya read these words, her face, which had been clouded with grief, turned radiant with joy, and she summoned the Ancient and smilingly said to him: " Ha! a veritable Branch from Hōrai this ; by my faith, let his false and trickful Highness be dismissed at once and take his Jewel-laden Branch with him ! "

The Ancient nodded assent, saying: "As the Branch is clearly a counterfeit, there need be no hesitation about returning it."

And with the Branch the Lady Kaguya, her heart now free of gloom, sent this stanza :

Makoto ka to	Was it the true branch of Hōrai
kikite mitsureba,	I asked as I gazed on thy gift :
koto no ha wo	mere leaves of sound (words)
kazareru tama no	were the jewels that adorned it,
yeda ni zo arikeru !	the Branch of Bloom thou
	broughtest me.

So was the False Branch returned to the Prince. The Ancient remembered the lying tale wherewith he had been beguiled, and regarded His Highness with anger, who meanwhile stood still a space, not knowing whether to go or stay. But as the sun sank deeper in the west, he bethought him again, and slunk off. Now the Lady Kaguya summoned the craftsmen who had caused this pother, and praised them, giving them ample largesse, whereat they rejoiced greatly, saying, thus they knew things would be, and departed. But on their way homewards they were set upon and punished by order of the Prince, blood was shed, and all their treasure was taken from them, and thus despoiled they fled and vanished. But His Highness felt he was put to unexampled shame, and his discomfiture threw a shadow over the remainder of his days. "Not only," he complained, " have I lost my mistress, but my name has become a reproach. throughout the land." Thereupon he fled to the deepest recesses of the hills, and dwelt there all the rest of his days. Times and again the chiefs and retainers of his household sought to discover their lord's retreat, but could not, and he

was as it were dead.   And it was out of this history of His
Highness Prince Kuramochi that arose the expression "tamazakaru." [1]

THE FLAME-PROOF FUR-ROBE.
(HI-NEZUMI NO KAWAGOROMO.)

The Sadaijin[2] Abe no Miushi[3] was a lord of wealth and
substance, and mighty withal.   In the year whereof we
speak, came to our country a merchant of Morokoshi,[4] by
name Wōkei,[5] on board a ship of that land, to whom was
indited a letter requiring him to buy for the Sadaijin a
fur-robe, which was said to exist, made of the pelt of the
Flame-proof Rat,[6] and Ono no Fusamori, one of the trustiest
of his lord's squires, was despatched in charge of the missive.
So Fusamori took the letter and went down to the coast,[7] and
delivered it to Wōkei, to whom he likewise gave gold.
Wōkei unrolled the scroll and read it, and made answer thus:
"The Flame-proof Fur-Robe is not to be obtained in my
country; men have talked of such a robe, but it has not been
seen.   If it exists anywhere, it is a thing that should assuredly
be brought to this land, but 'tis very hard to get by way of
trade.   Nevertheless, if by any hap such a robe has been
carried to India, the great merchants may be able to obtain
it, and should they fail, the gold now bestowed upon me
shall be returned to him who brought it, to hand back to the
Lord Sadaijin."
Upon the ship's return from the land of Morokoshi,

---

[1] An expression which may by taken to mean either, "blooming with jewels,"
or "preciously blooming," or again, *tamashii-zakaru*, "to have one's wits gone
a wool-gathering."

[2] *Sadaijin*, Left Great Minister, next in rank to the Daijōdaijin or Premier.

[3] In some texts Abe no Mimuraji. Mi-muraji is Great Chieftain, see Mr.
Chamberlain's translation of the Kojiki.

[4] An invented name. The characters are 王 卿.

[5] A common designation of China, even up to recent times. Its derivation is
uncertain.

[6] *Hi-nezumi. Nezumi* (root-gnawer or perhaps rice (ine) gnawer) is a generic
name for Rodents. In the legend is doubtless involved an allusion to the asbestos-
cloth mentioned in Colonel Yule's admirable work on Marco Polo, as a product
of the country lying north of China proper.

[7] Probably to Hakata in Chikuzen, a favourite resort of Chinese traders in
early times.

the Sadaijin, having tidings that Fusamori was on board and was making ready to come up to the capital, despatched a swift horse to meet him, so that he journeyed from Tsukushi to Miako in the short space of seven days.[1] Then a letter was delivered to the Sadaijin, who unrolled it and read these words: "The Flame-proof Fur-robe have I finally won, after great toil and the despatch of many men in quest thereof, for difficult it is to find now, as it was of old. Long ago a venerable priest from India brought such a robe into our land, and I heard that it was preserved in a certain temple lying among the remote western hills. I besought the aid of the ruler of the district, which was accorded me, and was allowed to purchase the robe, but the money was not sufficient, and fifty riyōs[2] of my own monies were added, which doubtless will be repaid to me ere the ship depart, or the Robe will be returned as pledge for the same." "Nay," cried the Sadaijin, "what is this talk about the gold; let the merchant have his gold without delay; welcome to me beyond words is the fruit of his quest." And turning his face towards the land of Morokoshi, he bowed him thrice, clasping his hands thankfully. Then, looking at the casket wherein the Fur-Robe was laid folded, he saw that it was beautifully adorned with inlaid work of various kinds of precious ruri,[3] and the Robe itself was of a glaucous[4] colour, the hairs tipped with shining gold, a treasure indeed of incomparable loveliness, more to be admired for its pure excellence than even for its virtue in resisting the flame of fire. "'Tis the very Robe, how pleased, methinks, the Lady Kaguya will be," cried the Sadaijin, and laid the Robe

---

[1] The distance is described as more than 900 *ri* (the Chinese *li* are meant) by the land route.

[2] Liang or taels, greatly exceeding in purchasing value, but to an extent not now definitely ascertainable, the tael or riyō of the present day.

[3] In the Commentary *ruri* is said to be a kind of precious stone that stands the fire, ten kinds of which are found within the famous 大 秦 國 Ta Ts'in country, supposed by some to be the Roman Empire, by others the countries lying west of China. Possibly varieties of turquoise or lapis lazuli are covered by the name. It has also been identified with the emerald, and Dr. Williams says it is the Sanskrit *Vaidurya*, which appears to be a sort of lapis lazuli.

[4] 錆. Probably a brilliant (lit. golden) shade of blue is meant. The Commentary explains the tint as superior to that of the sky 空 青.

carefully in the casket which he attached to a Branch of
Bloom; and putting on his fairest apparel,[1] and feeling
assured that the gift would win him his wooing, added a
scroll, whereon was writ a stanza, and carried the gift to the
Lady's abode.

Kagiri naki	Endless are the fires of love
omoi ni yakenu	that consume me, yet unconsumed
kawagoromo :	is the Robe of Fur :
tamoto kawakite	dry at last are my sleeves,
kiyō koso wa mime !	for shall I not see her face this day !

Thus cheering himself, the Sadaijin reached the entrance
of the Lady's dwelling, and the Ancient came out and took
the casket and bore it within to the Lady Kaguya. And she
gazed awhile upon the Robe and said :

"A fair robe of fur it seems to be, but till it be proved,
how can we know if it be not false."

But the Ancient answered :

"However that may be, deign to invite the Sadaijin to
enter ; the like of yonder Robe the world doth not appear
to hold ; be not so distrustful, daughter, nor drive men to
despair."

Then he went out and invited the Sadaijin to enter. And
now the Lady, though her heart was heavy, felt she must
receive him, for greatly as the Ancient had grieved over her
continued maidenhood, seeking ever to find her a worthy
mate, yet never had he sought to constrain her, seeing how
deeply she dreaded to give herself to any man.

But she said to the Ancient: "If this Robe be thrown
amid the flames and be not burnt up, I shall know it is in
very truth the Flame-proof Robe, and may no longer refuse
this lord's suit. As it has not its fellow in the world, and 'tis
averred to be, without doubt, the famous Robe that resists
flame, the proof may well be dared."

And the Ancient agreed, and told the Sadaijin it must be
so, whereupon he answered : " What doubt can there be—

---

[1] More literally, taking the greatest pains with his personal appearance, as if
he was going to a Court Levee—*on mi no kisō (keshō, ito itaku shite.*

even in the land of Morokoshi the Robe was not to be got, and could only be found after long and toilsome search; nevertheless, as the Lady will have it so, let the Robe be cast among the flames."

And a fire was kindled, and the Robe was flung therein and in a flash of flame perished utterly. So was it shown that it was not, in truth, made of the famous Flame-proof Fur. When the Sadaijin saw this, his face grew green as grass, and he stood there astonished. But the Lady Kaguya rejoiced exceedingly, and caused the casket to be returned with a scroll in it whereon was writ a verse :—

Nagori naku mo	Without a vestige even left
moyu to shiriseba,	thus to burn utterly away,
kawagoromo	had I dreamt it of this Robe of Fur,
omoi no hoka ni	Alas the pretty thing! far otherwise
okite mimashi wo!	would I have dealt with it.[1]

But the Sadaijin withdrew discomfited and shut himself up in his mansion. And men, hearing that Abe had accomplished his Quest and was abiding with the Lady Kaguya, inquired at the Lady's dwelling if that were so, and were told the fate of the Robe of Fur and that he abode not with the Lady, and hearing this they exclaimed "An *ahenashi*,[2] piece of work in truth, this fruitless job"

THE JEWEL IN THE DRAGON'S HEAD.

(TATSU NO KUBI NO TAMA.)

The Dainagon[3] Ōtomo no Miyuki,[4] being in his mansion, assembled his household and deigned to say: "In the head of the Dragon lies a jewel, rainbow-hued, and on him who

---

[1] There is a word-play here on the *i* (*hi*) of *omoi*, *hi* meaning 'flame.'

[2] *Ahenashi* (*ayenashi*), with *nigori*, *abenashi*. *Ayenashi* 敢 無 or 無 端 is a locution used of a bootless undertaking, something feeble, awkward and unsuccessful.

[3] *Dainagon*, Great Councillor, next in rank to the Udaijin, or Right Great Minister, who followed the Sadaijin.

[4] Ōtomo seems to mean many multitudes or companies of men. Miyuki—the personal name—is homophonous with the word signifying a Royal Progress or Promenade.

shall win it me shall nought remain unbestowed he may
desire." His men listened to their lord's words, and one
said humbly : " The high behests of our lord his servants
hear with trembling awe ; but how shall a mortal man light
upon such a jewel, or draw it forth from the head of a
Dragon ! " Whereto the Dainagon answered : " If ye call
yourselves the servants of your lord, even at the peril of your
lives are ye bound to do his bidding. The jewel whereof
I speak is not to be found in our land,[1] nor yet in the land
of Tenjiku, nor in that of Morokoshi ; the Dragon is
a monster that creeps up the hill-slopes from the sea
and rushes down them into the ocean [2]—but of what can
ye be thinking in shirking this Quest ? " And they said :
" As our lord wills, so must it be, and albeit the task were a
perilous one, we will not shirk it." Whereupon the Dainagon
regarded them with a smile, and cried, " Ye would not
surely put shame on your lord's name nor refuse to do his
bidding."

Then he dismissed them upon the Quest after the Dragon's
head gem, and that they might not want for food and
support on their way, endless store of silk and cotton and
coin and other things needful were bestowed upon them.
And the Dainagon promised that he would live in seclusion,
awaiting their return, and bade them not cast their looks
homewards until they had won the jewel. So they hearkened
humbly each of them and departed.

They were bidden to take the jewel from the Dragon's
head, but where to turn their steps they could not tell, and
they fell to reproaching their lord for being thus bewitched
by a fair face. Then they divided amongst them what had
been bestowed upon them, and some withdrew to their
houses, there to lie hid, while others went whither they

---

[1] That is, in none of the Sankoku (three countries, Japan, India, and China),
of which, in imitation of the Chinese Sankwoh, the civilized world was supposed
to consist.

[2] In some provinces, says the Commentary, the rivers, roaring down the
narrow valleys to the sea during the heavy rains, are supposed to be changed into
this particular form of Dragon, which has been seen to lift itself from the sea-
surface towards a descending cloud—an interpretation doubtless of the phenomena
attending the formation of a waterspout.

listed. 'Twas very well to be loyal to parent and prince, as the maxim runs, they muttered, but a behest so burdensome as this could not be obeyed, and bitterly they reproached their lord for having laid upon them such a task.

Meanwhile the Dainagon deeming his mansion common and mean, and unfit to receive the Lady Kaguya, caused it to be adorned throughout and made beautiful with curious lacquer-work in gold and silver, as well as with plain bright lacquer, and over the roof he ordered silken cloths of divers colours to be drawn, and every chamber to be hung with fine brocade, and the panels of the sliding partitions to be enriched with cunningly-wrought pictures, and the splendour of the mansion passed all description. And feeling sure that ere long he should obtain possession of the Lady Kaguya, he put away all the women of his household, and passed the days and the nights in solitude, and through the days and the nights awaited the return of his men; and so a year came and went, but still he heard no tidings of them. At last, weary of waiting, and sick at heart with the lack of news, he took two of his squires with him, and thus meanly served journeyed to Naniwa, and made inquiry there if any of his folk had taken boat in quest of the Dragon, to slay the monster and win the jewel that lay in his head; but the shipmen laughed and answered : " 'Tis a strange thing thou speakest of; on such a business be sure no boat has left this haven." Thereupon the Dainagon said to himself: " These be but silly, feeble ship-folk, how should they know aught of this matter? Myself I will take my bow and despatch this monster, and draw the jewel from his head, nor wait longer for these laggard fellows of mine." So he took a boat, and embarked in it, and fared over sea until the land lay far behind him, and still he caused the boat to be sculled on until his keel rode on the waters of distant Tsukushi. Then without any foresign the wind rose and the air darkened, and the craft was driven hither and thither, blown about by the gale; now it seemed as though the boat must founder in the trough of the sea, now great billows threatened to topple over and overwhelm it, while the thunder-god

thundered so appallingly that his monstrous drums seemed
to hang close overhead.   So the Dainagon lost heart, and
cried aloud, saying : " Never before have I been in such
perilous case, alas! what help may be invoked ? "   And the
helmsman answered: " Long have I voyaged in these waters,
yet so terrible an ill fortune as this never hath befallen me ;
if we sink not to the bottom of the sea, the thunder will
strike us; if by good hap the favour of the gods save us from
these perils, the gale will drive the boat far amid (the
barbarian islands of) the southern ocean ; woe worth the day
I took service with my lord of evil fate, where death, belike,
must be the wages ! "   And as he spoke the shipman burst
into tears.   But the Dainagon said :

"He who fares over sea must needs trust himself to the
helmsman, who should be steadfast as a high hill.   Why
speakest thou then thus despairfully?" and as he uttered
these words a terrible sickness came upon him.   Then the
helmsman answered : " Is your servant then a god that he
can render service now ?   The howling of the wind and the
raging of the waves and the mighty roar of the thunder
are signs of the wrath of the god whom my lord offends,
who would slay the dragon of the deep, for through the
dragon is the storm raised, and well it were if my lord
offered a prayer."

"Thou sayest wisely," answered the Dainagon, and he
fell to calling upon the god of seafolk, repenting him of his
frowardness and folly who had sought to slay the Dragon,
and vowing solemnly that never more would he strive to
harm so much as a hair of the great ruler of the deep.   A
thousand times he repeated his prayer, neither standing nor
sitting (but bowing him humbly before the god without
ceasing).   Then—was it not in answer to his prayer?—the
thunder died down and the gloom lifted, but still the wind
blew mightily.   " 'Tis the Dragon's handiwork," said the
helmsman after a while, " a fair wind blows now, and drives
the boat swiftly towards our own land."   But the Dainagon
could not understand him.   For three or four days the bark
sped before the wind till land came in sight, and they saw

it was the strand of Akashi in Harima.   Nevertheless the
Dainagon would not be persuaded they had not been blown
southwards on some savage shore, and lay motionless and
panting in the bottom of the boat, nor would he rise, when
the governor of the district, to whom his squires had sent
tidings of their lord's misadventure, presented himself.   But
under the pine trees that overshadowed the beach mats were
spread, whereupon the Dainagon saw it was on no savage
shore they had drifted, and he roused himself and got on land.
And when the governor saw him, he could not forbear smiling
at the wretched appearance of the discomfited lord, chilled to
the very bone, with swollen belly and eyes lustreless as sloes.
But the proper orders were given, and a litter got ready in
which the Dainagon was borne slowly to his mansion.   Then
those of his followers whom he had sent upon the Quest
got wind somehow of their lord's return, and presented
themselves humbly before him, saying : " We have failed
in our quest, and have lost all claim to an audience, but
now 'tis known how terribly hard was the task imposed,
and hither have we ventured to come, and we trust that a
gracious forbearance will be extended and that we shall not
be driven out of our lord's following."

The Dainagon went out to receive them and said : " Ye
have done well to return, even empty-handed.   Yonder
Dragon, assuredly, has kinship with the Thunder-God, and
whoever shall lay hands on him to take the jewel that
gleams in his head shall find himself in parlous peril.
Myself am sore spent with toil and hardship, and no guerdon
have I won.   A thief of men's souls, and a destroyer of their
bodies, is the Lady Kaguya, nor ever will I seek her abode
again, nor ever bend ye your steps thitherwards."

Then the Dainagon took what was left of his substance,
and divided it among those whom he had bidden go in
quest of the Jewel.   And when his women, whom he had
dismissed, heard of his misadventure, they laughed till their
sides were sore, while the silken cloths he had caused to
be drawn over the roof of his mansion were carried away,
thread by thread, by the crows to line their nests with.

And when men asked whether the Dainagon Ōtomo had won the Dragon-Jewel, they were answered: "Not so, but his eyeballs are become two jewels very like a pair of sloes,[1] nor other jewels has he won." "Ana! tayegata,"[2] was the reply, and thus the expression first arose.

THE ROYAL HUNT.

(MI-KARI NO MIYUKI.)

Meanwhile the fame of the incomparable loveliness of the Lady Kaguya had reached the Court, and the Mikado caused one of the palace dames, Fusago by name, to be summoned, and said to her: "Of many a man has the strange beauty of this Kaguya been the ruin ; go thou, therefore, and see what manner of damsel the girl be."

The Dame heard and departed, and came to the dwelling of the Bamboo-Hewer, where she was courteously received by the goodwife and invited to enter. " 'Tis at the bidding of His Majesty I have journeyed hither, who has heard that the beauty of the Lady Kaguya passes all description, and has commanded me to seek audience of her."

So spoke she and the goodwife answered, "Your servant will humbly repeat your message," and sought the inner apartment, and prayed the maiden to receive the Palace Dame. But she would not, for that she was no wise beautiful, she said. Then the goodwife chided her for her churlish speech, and inquired how she dared treat thus rudely the King's message. But the Lady Kaguya still refused to receive the Dame, saying that His Majesty showed little wisdom in despatching one of his ladies upon such an errand. Nor might the Ancient nor his goodwife constrain her, for though she filled the place of a child born to them, ever she held herself aloof from the ways of the world. So the goodwife sought again the Palace Dame, and said, " Pity 'tis, but of so tender years

---

[1] *Sumomo.* Chinese 李 opposed to the 桃, the peach, symbol of beauty and plumpness.

[2] *Tayegata (tahegata)* means 'insupportable' but with *nigori (tabegata)*, uneatable. The Dainagon had got his eyeballs swollen like sloes, and these were uneatable fruits, for his pains.

is our daughter she may not venture to meet a Lady of the Court." But the Dame answered, not without some anger : "The Damsel may not be excused, for His Majesty has bidden me see her, and how can I return without fulfilling the Royal behest? Will she set at nought the commands of the Ruler of the Land, and so be guilty of an unexampled folly?"

Still the Lady Kaguya willed not to give audience to the Palace Dame, saying : "I cannot yield obedience in this matter, if need be, let me be put to death."

And the Dame thereupon returned to the Palace, and made report of what had occurred.

"Verily," said His Majesty, "I can well believe 'tis a woman who revels in the destruction of men." So after a pause, thinking over the matter, the Mikado concluded that she must be constrained to yield due obedience, and caused the Ancient to be summoned to the Palace, to whom was conveyed this command. "A daughter thou hast, Kaguya by name, whom we bid thee bring to us. Fair of face and form we have heard she is, and we sent one of our Ladies to see her, but she would not be seen. How comes it our will is thus disdainfully received in thy house?"

To which the Ancient answered humbly : "It is true the child willed not to become a Lady of the Palace, and caused your servant sore grief, but he will hasten back to his dwelling and lay your Majesty's gracious commands upon her." To which was deigned the reply : "How! has not the Ancient reared the child, and may she oppose his will? Let the Maiden be brought hither, and a hat of nobility, perchance, shall be her father's reward."

The Ancient rejoiced greatly at hearing this, and returned to his dwelling, and conveyed the Royal command to the Lady Kaguya, bidding her no longer refuse obedience. But she said : "Never will I serve His Majesty as 'tis desired ; and if constraint be used towards your daughter, she will pine away and die, and the price of my father's hat of nobility will be the destruction of his child."

"Nay, die thou shalt not," cried the Ancient ; "what were

a hat of nobility to me if never again I beheld thee? Yet,
daughter, I pray thee, tell thy father why thou refusest to
become a Lady of the Palace and why shouldest thou die if
thou shouldest serve his Majesty?"

"Empty words seem thy daughter's," answered the
Damsel, "but true will they prove if she be constrained to
do this thing. Many a suitor has wooed her, lords of no
mean estate, who nevertheless have been dismissed, and
should she listen to his Majesty, her name would become a
reproach among men."

Then the Ancient answered: "Little care I for matters of
state, but thy days must know no peril, nor shalt thou be in
any wise constrained, and I will hasten to the palace and
humbly represent to His Majesty that thou mayest not become
an inmate thereof.

Thereupon he went up to the Capital, and represented that
the Lady Kaguya, after hearing the Royal Command, nevertheless willed not to become a Lady of the Palace, and might
not be constrained without peril of her life; and further,
that she was not the born child of Miyakko Maro, but had
been found by him one day when hewing bamboos on the
hill-side, and that she was in ways and moods of other
fashion than the fashion of this world. Upon this being
reported to his Majesty, he said: "Dwells not this Miyakko
Maro among the hills hard by our capital? Let a Royal
Hunt be ordered, and, perchance, thus we may gain a glimpse
of the Maiden."

The Ancient, when the Royal pleasure was made known
to him, said: "'Tis an excellent device; thus may his
Majesty, without difficulty, on the Hunt being unexpectedly
ordered, gain a glimpse of the Lady Kaguya ere a thought
of it enters her heart."

So a day was appointed, and the Royal Hunt ordered, and
the Mikado watched for an opportunity and entered the
Bamboo-Hewer's dwelling. And as the threshold was
crossed, it was seen that the house was filled with light, and
midmost the glory stood a Being. "Ha! 'tis the Lady,"
cried the Mikado, and drew nigh, but she made to fly, and a

royal hand was laid upon her sleeve, and she covered her face, but not with such swiftness that a glimpse of it was not caught, and the loveliness of it was seen to be incomparable. And His Majesty would fain have led her forth, but she stood there and spoke these words: "No liege of your Majesty is his servant, and she may not therefore be thus led away." But it was answered that she must not resist the Royal Will, and a palace litter approached, whereupon of a sudden the Lady dissolved in thin air and vanished. The monarch stood dumb with astonishment, and understood that the Lady was of no mortal mould, and said : " It shall be as thou desirest, Maiden ; but 'tis prayed that thou resume thy form, that once more thy beauty may be seen."

So she resumed her form and the glory of her loveliness filled the Royal heart with overwhelming delight ; and graciously was the Ancient remembered, through whom this joy had come to His Majesty, and upon him was bestowed the rank of Chief of the Hiyak'kwan.[1]

But great was the grief that the Lady willed not to dwell in the Palace, and as the Monarch was about to be borne away, it seemed as if the Royal soul was being left behind, and a stanza was composed whereof the words were these :

Kayeru sa no	Mournful the return
miyuki mono uku	of the Royal Hunt,
omohoyete ;	and full of sorrow the broooding heart ;
somukite tomaru	for she resists and stays behind,
Kaguya Hime yuye !	the Lady Kaguya !

And the Lady answered thuswise :—

Mugura hafu	Under the roof o'ergrown with hopbine
shimo ni mo toshi wa	long were the years
tōrinuru mi no ;	she passed,
nanika wa tama no	how may she dare to look upon
utena wo mo mimu !	the Palace of Precious Jade ?

---

[1] Here Chief of the Mikado's Retinue :—it was, however, merely an honorary, not a real appointment.

When the answer was read, more than ever was the Monarch disinclined to go back bootless to the Palace, and long the litter was delayed, for no resolve could be come to, until it seemed at last as though the dawn would be there waited for through the night; whereupon reluctantly' was the order given to return. But the Ladies of the Court were disdained, for their beauty paled before that of the Lady Kaguya, aye the fairest of them, when compared with her image, lost all her charms. Only on the Lady could the Royal heart dwell, and on none other, and the apartments of the Palace Dames were abandoned and desolate, sad to say! while letter after letter was sent to the Lady Kaguya, who answered them not ungently,[1] and verses were composed and fairly writ on scrolls attached to posies, and interchanged, and thus the days passed by.

THE CELESTIAL ROBE OF FEATHERS.[2]

(AME NO HA-GOROMO.)

So in the Palace and in the Hut was consolation attained; and three years went by, when, in the early spring, the Lady Kaguya fell to gazing upon the shining orb of the rising moon, and a brooding sadness seemed to take possession of her. She was counselled not thus ceaselessly to contemplate the face of the moon, for so was bred mournfulness; but she still in solitude watched the orb, until tears of grief ran down her cheeks in floods. Then, on the mid-month day of the seventh month rose the full moon, and unutterable grew the misery, and the maidens who served the Lady sought the Ancient and said: "Long has the Lady Kaguya watched the moon, waxing in melancholy with the waxing thereof, and her woe now passes all measure, and sorely she weeps and wails; wherefore we counsel thee to speak with her."

---

[1] "Go henji sasuga ni nikukarazu kikoyekawashitamaite."
[2] The fifth quest – that of the Lord of Iso – is omitted, principally on account of its triviality and lack of interest. A brief account of it will be found in the concluding portion of this article.

And the Ancient went to her and said : " What hast thou on thy mind, daughter, that ever thou gazest thus sadly on yonder moon's pallid face ? Lackest thou aught that may be needed for thy happiness ? "

But she answered : " As I gaze upon the moon I am sad because my heart is broken as I consider the wretchedness of this world."

And deeper grew her melancholy each time the Ancient visited her chamber, till sorrow-struck by her distress, he said : " Ah ! my darling, my Buddha, why broodest thou thus ? what grief oppresses thee ? "

" 'Tis no grief, save the grief that breaks my heart because of the wretchedness of the world."

" Watch yonder moon no more, daughter ; ever art thou gazing upon it, and thus thy woe deepens."

" How may I cease, father, to gaze upon the orb ! " said the Lady, and still she watched the moon from its rising to its setting, her face wet with tears the while ; but when the nights were moonless,[1] her woe departed from her. Yet as the new moon came and waxed again, the Lady wailed and wept, and her women whispered among themselves that ever deeper grew the misery ; but they could not learn the secret of her woe, neither could the Ancient. So the eighth month came in due course, and when the moon was at its full the Lady wept floods of tears, nor essayed she to hide her grief. And again and again her foster-parents prayed her to tell them the cause of her wretchedness. The Lady yielded to their prayer, and said, weeping sorely the while : " Again and again have I willed to tell you all, but I felt assured your hearts would be wrung with grief by my words, and therefore have I forborne till now; and now is the hour come I may no longer abide with you. No maid of this mortal land am I, but the Capital of Moonland is my birth-place. Long ago it was decreed that I should descend upon this earth, and bide there somewhile ; but now is the time at hand when I must go back whence I came, for when yonder orb shall be

---

[1] After the 21st day of the month, explains the Commentary.

at its fullest, a company of moonfolk will come down from
the sky to bear me away. Well I knew this was my doom,
and now ye can understand my misery and wherefore I
have wept and wailed so sorely since the spring followed
winter."

And as the Lady spoke, again the tears flowed in abundance down her cheeks. But the Ancient said : " What thing
is this thou speakest, daughter? I found thee, 'tis true, in the
hollow of a bamboo, but no bigger wert thou than a rape-
seed, and have we not cherished thee while thou grewest up
to full maidenhood? None dare take thee from us, by heaven!
I will not let thee go."

And he clamoured, amid his tears, that he was like to die ;
unbearably piteous 'twas to see his misery. But the Lady
answered : " My father and my mother are still numbered
among the dwellers in yonder Moonland's capital. It was
but for a while I came down to earth, and now many a year
has gone by since you found me. So long have I dwelt
among you that I have forgotten my father and my mother,
and now I look upon you as though I were your very
child ; nor indeed would I fain do otherwise than remain
with you, but, though terrible to me is the thought of
quitting you, I may not flee my fate." And she fell to
weeping, and the old folk wept also, and her women who
had tended her through so many years and watched her
grow up into perfect beauty, now hearing they must lose her
whom they loved so well, could not swallow their tears, and,
oppressed by a like woe, were consumed with grief.

Now the Mikado, hearing of these things, sent a messenger
to the Hewer's dwelling, and the Ancient came out to receive
him, weeping abundantly. So bitter had been his grief that
his hair had turned white, and his limbs become bowed, and
his eyes blear, and though his years were but fifty,[1] he
seemed as if his woe had all at once turned him into an
old man.

The messenger inquired if the tidings which had reached

---

[1] He has previously been described as a man of seventy. The Commentary
treats the question with befitting gravity in a long note.

His Majesty as to the cause of the Hewer's distress were true, and the Ancient, still weeping, answered:

"At the full moon a company from the Moonland capital will come down to bear away our daughter. Deeply grateful am I to His Majesty, who deigns to make inquiry about this matter, and I humbly represent that if at the time of full moon a guard of soldiers be granted us, these Moonfolk, if they make their raid, may all be captured."

The messenger thereupon returned, and reported to the Mikado the plight wherein he found the Ancient.

And the Mikado said: "But a passing glimpse have I had of the Lady Kaguya, yet never shall I lose the memory of her exceeding loveliness; how hard then must it be for those who are wont to see her morning and evening to lose her!" So orders were given that the captains should be ready by the full moon, and the General Taka no Ōkuni was commanded to take a thousand men from each of the Left and Right Regiments of Royal Guards to protect the Hewer's dwelling against the raid of the Moonfolk. When the two thousand soldiers reached the Ancient's abode, one moiety was posted around it on the earth platform whereon it stood, and the other moiety on the roof of the house, all with bow bent and arrow on string, while the men of the household too were arrayed, and so many were the defenders that no spot remained unguarded, and even within the dwelling the women kept watch and ward, while the Lady was placed in the store-house, surrounded by her attendants, the door whereof the Ancient bolted, and posted himself outside thereof, saying: "Watch and ward thus strict, even Heavenfolk may not win through," and crying to the soldiers on the roof to look out for the first sign of a swoop being made through the air, and slay whatever creature might in this way approach them, whereto they answered: "Have no care, so keen our watch not even a bat shall escape our artillery, and due exposure of its head, by way of punishment, should it venture near our ranks."

And the Ancient was greatly comforted by these words, but the Lady Kaguya said: "Though ye thus surround me

and protect me and make ye ready to fight for me, yet ye
cannot prevail over the folk of yonder land, nor will your
artillery harm them nor your defences avail aught against
them, for every door will fly open at their approach, nor may
your valour help, for be ye never so stout-hearted, when the
Moonfolk come, vain will be your struggle with them."

Then the Ancient was angered, and shouted : "If these
Moonfolk come, my nails shall turn into talons to claw out
their eyes. I will seize them by their forelocks and twist them
off, and trample upon them ; their hinder-parts will I tear to
pieces; to shame will I put them before the face of these
Royal warmen."

But the Lady said: "Make not so great a clamour, lest
the warmen hear thee, which were unseemly. Ere long,
alas ! I shall no longer be within your love, ere long I must
know the bitterness of parting, nor can I ever return to show
my love and gratitude, for closed to me will be the world's
ways. When I went out month after month to watch the
waxing moon, I prayed for yet another year to bide with
you; but the boon was refused me, and I could but wail and
weep as ye saw me. I have beguiled your hearts to love me,
and now must quit you ; alas, alas ! Of that pure essence
are these Moonfolk that they know not old age nor ever
suffer from any pain or grief, yet fain would I abide with
my foster-parents; terrible it is to me to think that ye will
grow old with no child to cherish you." So saying, the
Lady wept sorely, but the Ancient, restraining his grief, said :

"Nay, daughter, thou must not anger beings so lovely as
those thou speakest of."

Meanwhile, the night wore away, and, at the hour of the
Rat, behold ! a glory fell about the dwelling that exceeded
the splendour of noon and was ten times as bright as the
brightness of the full moon, so that the smallest hair-pore
could be seen on the skin. In the midst thereof came down
through the air a company of angels riding on a coil of cloud
that descended until it hovered some cubits' height above the
ground. And there the angels stood ranked in due order ;
and when the warmen on guard saw them, a great fear fell

PHOTO-LITH.

8 THE UPBEARING OF THE LADY KAGUYA

upon them, upon those without as upon those within the dwelling, and they had no stomach for fighting. But after a while they rallied; and some bent the bow, but the strength departed from their arms, and they were as though stricken with palsy; and mightier men let fly anon, but the shafts went all astray, and these too could not fight, and thus feeble and bootless proved the vaunted watch and ward of the Royal Warmen.

In shining garments were the angels clad, that had not their like under heaven, and in the midst of them, as they stood in serried ranks upon the cloud, was seen a canopied car hung with curtains of finest woollen fabric, where sat One who seemed to be their lord. And the Archangel turned towards the Hewer's abode, and cried out in a loud voice, "Come thou forth, Miyakko Maro." And the Hewer came forth, staggering like a drunken man, and fell on his face prostrate.

Then the Archangel said, "Thou fool! Some small virtue didst thou display in thy life, and to reward thee was this maiden sent to bide with thee somewhile, and years and years hath she dwelt under thy ward, and heaps and heaps of gold have been bestowed upon thee, and thou hast as it were become a new man. To expiate a fault she had committed was the Lady Kaguya doomed to bide a little while in thy wretched home, and now is the doom fulfilled, and we are come to bear her away from thine earth. Vain is thy weeping and lamentation, render up the girl and delay not."

Then the Ancient answered humbly, "For over a score of years thy servant has cherished the maiden, whereof his lord speaks strangely as being but a little while. Perchance the Lady whom his lord would bear away with him dwells elsewhere; the Lady Kaguya who bides beneath this roof is very sick and may not leave her chamber."

No answer was vouchsafed, but the Car was borne upwards on the cloud till it hovered over the houseroof and a voice cried, "Ho there, Kaguya! how long wouldest thou tarry in this sorry place?"

3

Thereupon the outer door of the storehouse, wherein stood the Lady Kaguya, flew open and the inner lattice-work, untouched by any hand, slid back and the Lady was seen in the light of the doorway, surrounded by her women, who, understanding that her departure could no longer be stayed, lifted up their hands and wept. But the Lady passed out, and drew nigh to where lay the Hewer, grovelling on the ground, weeping and stunned with grief, and said : "My fate bids me, father ; will you not follow me with your eyes as I am borne away ?"

But the Hewer answered : "Why in my misery should I follow thee with my eyes ? Let it be done unto me as may be listed, let me be left desolate, let these angels who have come down from the sky to fetch thee bear thee thither with them." And the Ancient refused to be comforted. Then the Lady indited a scroll, seeing that her foster-father was too overcome with grief to listen to her words, and left it to be given him after she had gone, weeping sorely and saying that when her father should yearn after his daughter, the words she had written should be read. And these were the words she wrote : "Had I been born in this land, never should I have quitted it until the time came for my father to suffer no sorrow for his child;[1] but now, on the contrary, must I pass beyond the boundaries of this world, though sorely against my will. My silken mantle I leave behind me as a memorial, and when the moon lights up the night, let my father gaze upon it; now my eyes must take their last look, and I must mount to yonder sky, whence I fain would fall meteor-wise to earth."

Now the Angels brought with them a coffer, wherein were contained a Celestial Feather Robe and a joint of bamboo filled with the Elixir of Life, and one of them said to the Lady Kaguya : "Taste, I pray you, of this Elixir, for soiled has your spirit become with the grossnesses of this filthy world."

---

[1] An euphemistic phrase hinting at her longing to remain with her father till death took him, and her fate could no longer grieve him.

Then the Lady tasted of the Elixir, and would have privily wrapt up a portion in the mantle she was leaving behind, as a memorial of her; but an Angel stayed her, and drawing forth the Celestial Robe, made ready to throw it over her shoulders, whereupon she said: "Have patience yet awhile; who dons yonder robe changes his heart, and I have still somewhat to say ere I depart." And again she fell to writing, and an Angel said: "'Tis late, and you delay, Lady, overmuch." But she rebuked him, and before all, mournfully and composedly, she wrote on; and the words she wrote were these:

"Your Majesty deigned to send a host to protect your servant, but it was not to be, and now is the misery at hand of departing with those who have come to bear her away with them. Not permitted was it to her to serve your Majesty, and maugre her will was it that she yielded not obedience to the Royal Command, and wrung with grief is her heart thereat, and perchance your Majesty may have thought the Royal will was not understood, and was opposed by her, and so will she appear to your Majesty lacking in good manners, which she would not your Majesty deemed her to be, and therefore humbly she lays this writing at the Royal Feet. And now must she don the Feather Robe and mournfully bid her lord farewell." Then when she had finished writing the scroll, the captain of the host was called, and it was delivered over, together with the bamboo joint containing the Elixir, into his hands, and as he took it, the Feather Robe was thrown over the Lady Kaguya, and in a trice, all memory of her foster-father's woe vanished, for those who don yonder Robe know sorrow no more. Then the Lady entered the car, surrounded by the company of Angels, and mounted skywards, while the Hewer and his Dame and the women who had served the Lady shed tears of blood, and stood stunned with grief; but there was no help. And the scroll left for the Ancient was read to him, but he said:

"What have I to live for? a bitter old age is mine. Of what profit is my life? whom have I to love?" Nor would he take of the Elixir, but lay prostrate on the ground and would not rise.

Meanwhile the Captain of the host returned to the capital with his men, and reported how vain had been the attempt to stay the departure of the Lady Kaguya, and all that had occurred, and gave the scroll, together with the bamboo joint containing the Elixir, to be laid before the Mikado. And His Majesty unrolled the scroll and read it, and was greatly moved, nor would take food nor any diversion. After a while a Grand Council was summoned, and it was inquired which among the mountains of the land towered highest towards heaven. And one said: "In Suruga stands a mountain, not remote from the capital, that towers highest towards heaven among all the mountains of the land." Whereof His Majesty being informed composed a stanza:

Au koto mo,	Never more to see her !
namida ni ukabu	Tears of grief overwhelm me,
waga mi ni wa ;	and as for me,
shinanu kusuri wa	with the Elixir of Life
nani ni ka wa semu ?	what have I to do ?

And the scroll together with the Elixir was given into the hands of one of the ladies of the palace, and she was charged to deliver them to one Tsuki no Iwakasa, with the injunction to bear them to the summit of the highest mountain in Suruga, that there, standing on the top of the highest peak thereof, he should cause the scroll and the Elixir to be consumed with fire.

So Tsuki no Iwakasa heard humbly the Royal Command, and took with him a company of warriors, and climbed the mountain and did as he had been bidden. And it was from that time forth that the name of Fuji[1] was given to yonder mountain, and men say that the smoke of that burning still curls from its high peak to mingle with the clouds of Heaven.

---

[1] One among the many ways of writing Fuji (*Fusiyama*) was 不 死, Immortal.

4 THE PASS OF GOKANYA (NANAOZAK FUJISAN FROI

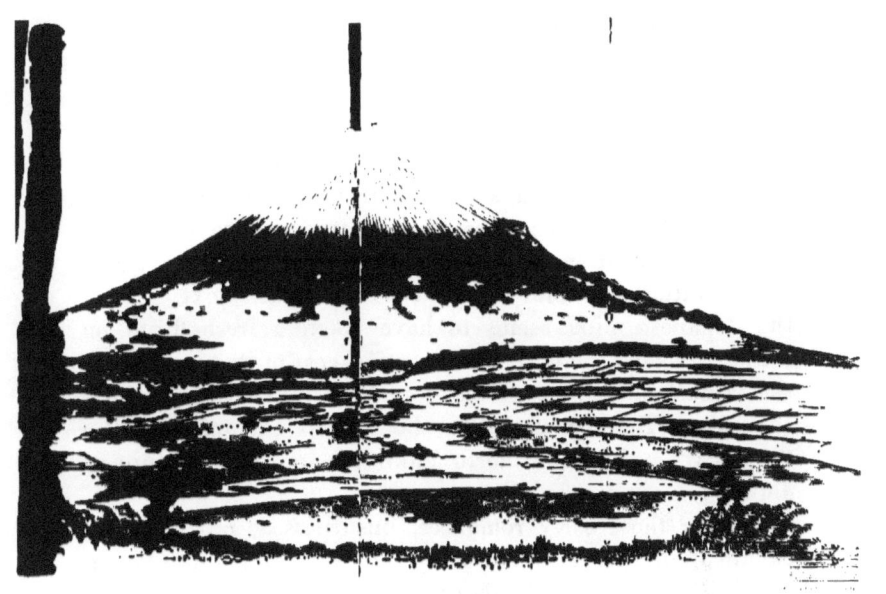

Japanese literature begins with the *Kojiki*[1] or Record of Ancient Matters, which appeared in A.D. 712. During the eighth and ninth centuries various works were produced, none of which, if we except the Anthologies, have any claim to admiration on literary grounds. But in the next century the Japanese mind seems to have taken a fresh flight, or rather to have awakened to a consciousness of its powers, and the remarkable series of *monogatari* or romances, of which the Tale of Taketori is at once the earliest example and the type, gave a lustre hitherto unknown to the literature of Japan.

Among these early romances, unsurpassed, probably unequalled, in literary quality, by the later fiction of Japan, the *Genji-monogatari*[2] holds the chief place in the estimation of native critics, who scarcely condescend to notice the Hewer's simple and tender story. To European readers, however, the record of Genji's love-adventures soon becomes wearisome, despite the clever dialogues upon the virtues and failings of women regarded as ministers to men's sensuous or æsthetic pleasures that relieve the monotony of the narrative—dialogues, by the way, that wear a strangely modern air, and might, with a few necessary changes, be transported bodily into a drawing-room novel of nineteenth-century London.

In the sense in which Shakespeare is said to have had little invention, the nameless author of the *Taketori* lacked originality. Most of the materials of his story are drawn from Chinese or Sinico-Indian sources. It could hardly

---

[1] This extraordinary farrago of feeble and often filthy myths and legends has had the good fortune to meet with so able a translator as Mr. B. H. Chamberlain. Trivial, even childish, as the collection is, it is interesting as furnishing striking instances of what myths in their crude beginnings really were. In addition, the traits of a fairly ample picture of the social life of the unsinicized Japanese may be gathered from it, and the songs it contains, though devoid of literary value, have considerable philological interest. Mr. Chamberlain has enriched his version with notes and commentaries that constitute an invaluable aid to the study of the origins of Dai Nippon.

[2] Many chapters of this history of a Japanese Don Juan have been recently translated by Mr. Suyematsu.

have been otherwise, for even as early as the tenth century
the legends and traditions of his country had been either
replaced by Chinese myths or recast in a Chinese mould,
and, excepting in the Rituals of Shinto, and some of the
songs quoted in the *Kojiki* or collected in the Anthologies,
all vestiges of the unwritten literature of primitive Japan
seem to have been lost. But the art and grace of the story
of the Lady Kaguya are native, its unstrained pathos, its
natural sweetness, are its own, and in simple charm and
purity of thought and language it has no rival in the fiction
either of the Middle Kingdom or of the Dragon-Fly Land.
The tags of word-plays that close the tale of each Quest are,
I cannot but believe, the additions of later hands, and I am
loth to look upon the story of the fifth Quest[1] as other
than the broad farce of some manipulator of a coarser period.
Perhaps, indeed, the Moon-maiden's story stood originally
alone, the work of some pious but not too orthodox Buddhist,
who shaped a Taouist legend into an allegory exemplifying
the great doctrine of *inguwa,* or Cause and Effect, in the
maiden's recovery of her celestial home through subduance
of the very feeling the indulgence of which had led her to
exile, despite the circumstance that a Mikado sought to
inspire, and a father to foster, the tender sentiment. In
such a story the narratives of the Quests may have been
afterwards interpolated, partly to display more fully the
maiden's constancy and purity, partly by way of gentle

---

[1] The Chiunagon Marotada has to present the Lady with a Cowry shell
(*Koyasugai*) brought by a swallow, *tsubakurame*, probably the *Hirundo gutturalis,*
Scop., which, according to Messrs. Blakiston and Pryer, nests always in a house,
where a shelf is provided for its accommodation. He has recourse to his retainers,
who devise various schemes, more or less trivial and ridiculous, in pursuance of
one of which the Chiunagon endeavours to catch a swallow sitting upon its nest
and in the act of wagging its tail. Thus far he is successful, but only to be
rewarded by a ball of dung, which he grasps firmly in his hand, believing he has
obtained the much-desired prize. In being lowered from his post of observation,
to which he had been raised in a sort of basket attached by a rope, he meets with
a mishap, and falls into a rice cauldron, from which his retainers drag him out
still grasping his supposed prize—the nature of which he then, to his stupefaction,
discovers.

The *Koyasugai* is described in the *Wakan sanzai* as the shell currency of
ancient China. The word is often written 子 安, under a false notion of its
etymology—probably *Koyasu* is a strengthened form of the root *Koye,* to bring
over, import, etc.

satire upon the taste for love-adventures which all the early romances show to have characterized the peaceful age, when neither Hei nor Gen had yet raised the stormy din of factious arms.

To render literally an Oriental text involves the effacement of whatever charm the original may possess.[1] I have therefore sought to give an English dress to the ideas, rather than to the mere language of the teller of this old-world story, probably the most ancient work of fiction extant of the whole Altaic race. But I have desired, at the same time, to preserve in the version as much as possible of the spirit, as distinct from the structure, of the unsinicized tongue of early Japan; and with this object have reproduced, to some extent, the loosely composite paragraph and sentence characteristic of Japanese prose, and abhorred of Chinese writers, who delight in a terse and antithetic, but bald and artificial style, that too commonly sacrifices wit to an obscure brevity, and loses all naturalness in the strain after mere symmetry of literary form. I have endeavoured, also, to retain the impersonality which so markedly differentiates Turanian[2] from Aryan speech; but I have usually found this possible only so far as it resulted from avoidance of metaphorical forms of expression. Of the numerous word-plays that disfigure the text I have not attempted any explanation unless needed to give some definite meaning to the passages where they occur. The 'honorifics' in Japanese have often little more than a pronominal value, and I have not been careful to translate them when not used to emphasize respect. The word 'mi' is the honorific commonly employed in the text in relation to the Mikado, and is usually rendered

<hr />

[1] An Italian version of the *Taketori* has been made by M. Severini, which I cannot greatly praise. It has also been translated into German, and through German into English. Of these latter versions I have seen neither. The present is, I believe, the first direct translation into English that has been produced, and the only one based on Daishu's text, or annotated with any approach to adequacy.

[2] On this peculiar feature of Turanian languages the reader is referred to some excellent observations by Mr. Lowell in his Chosön or Land of Morning Calm (Korea). Mr. Aston, too, has some admirable remarks on the subject in a paper on the Korean and Japanese languages, which will be found in Vol. XI. Part III. of this Journal.

'imperial' or 'august,' expressions to which I have preferred
the simpler 'royal.'   In his preface Tanaka Daishu (the
Sinico-Japanese pronunciation of the characters with which
Ōhide is written) says that if you read the *Taketori* over
lightly, it will seem quite easy to understand; but if you want
to 'taste' it, you will find it no easy matter thoroughly to
comprehend it, not only because the style is antique and
concise, but because by dint of frequent copying the text is
not unfrequently corrupt.   I have experienced to the full
the justice of these remarks, and am less certain now of the
accuracy of many passages in my translation than I was at
the beginning of my task ; it was only after prolonged study
of the text that I found I did not always fully 'taste' it.

Japanese art has but rarely drawn its motives from the
scenes of the Tale of Taketori.   The earliest edition I have
met with is illustrated with coarse woodcuts, but these are
destitute of all merit.   My friend M. Philippe Burty, however, possesses the concluding roll of an illuminated *makimono,* which he has kindly lent me, and the second of the
three chromo-lithographs, with which I have been allowed to
illustrate this translation—the Upbearing of Kaguya—is a
reduced reproduction of its last scene.   The two remaining
chromo-lithographs are taken from *makimonos* in my own
possession ; the View of Fujisan from a roll bearing the title
Sanka rekishōzu, a Series of Pictures of Hills and Streams,
and the other, which I have called The Oread's Haunt, from
a roll that is partly calligraphic and partly a copy of a
Chinese painting.   The latter roll is contained in a case of
black persimmon wood (*Diospyros kaki*), superscribed *Tōgen
senseki,* 桃 源 仙 蹟, and on the silk lining of its lid is a
legend written in Chinese by the copyist, of which the subjoined version may be found interesting :—

"Hath any mortal, pray you, ever trod the streamy
domains where the Fairy's[1] peach-tree blooms ?   Now the

---

[1] The Chinese Oread (仙), Si Wang Mu, the Western Royal Mother, who on
Mount Kwenlun rules over thousands of Taoist genii. A peach-tree growing within
her domain on the borders of the Gem Lake (瑤 池) bears fruits which confer
immortality upon those who are allowed by the Mother to partake of them.

sage Tōrei (陶 今) beheld the wickedness of the world, and his heart was sore within him, and he fled from men, and made his abode among the Eastern wilds, and the gates of the Fairies' domain were opened to him, and in that mystic land untrodden by foot of man he gained the fruits of creative energy. To Meichō (明 趙[1]), whose days were when the Ming ruled, came the fame of the adventure of Tōrei, and he bethought him and wrought a picture, and depicted the high hills rising endlessly one above the other, and many a dizzy precipice, and the mulberry bush and the hemp plant, and fair to behold was the varied scene. There, too, were upland fields and valley rice-lands, and amidst them was seen the humble thatch of the husbandman. It was cunningly limned, one might liken it to fine needlework or the tracery of a patterned fabric. And in the course of time the scroll was brought within the borders of Kishiu, and my lord begged the loan of it, and at my lord's behest I made this copy of the picture. Though the scroll has been borne over the surging sea, amid roaring gales, over wild passes and streamy hills, and has been in peril from fire and struggle of armed men, and from tooth of rat and gnaw of worm, as from harm by spear or arrow, yet has no hurt come to it, for the gods and demons, I trow, have ever watched over its safety, during the many hundred years that have passed since it was wrought. Fair is the retreat among the wild hills, by the lintels of the door waves a willow, hard by the chrysanth blows, and a little beyond a pine-tree overshadows the meeting of three ways. Who shall now say that never have the gates of the Fairy Domain been thrown open to mortals? Written on a forenoon, in the second month of the second year of Ansei (A.D. 1855-6), at Sanke (?), within the province of Kishiu, by Kikuchi Tōsei."

As the legend of Mount Hōrai (P'êng lai) is, doubtless,

Kwenlun is by some identified with the range of mountains known as the Hindu Kush (see Mayers' Chinese Readers' Manual, p. 108), and the legend is evidently in great part of Indian origin.

[1] Not to be confounded with the Japanese *Meichō* 明 徑 .

intimately connected, in part at least, with that of Si Wang
Mu, I have used a portion of Chao's picture, no adequate
representation of the Island Mountain being known to me,
as fairly conveying the Sinico-Japanese idea of the fabled
Immortal Isle of the Eastern Ocean.[1]

In the third volume of the *Gunsho ichiran* (a Japanese
bibliography published about the year 1800), the early
monogatari, among which the Hewer's tale holds the first
place in merit as in time, are enumerated and briefly noticed,
often with a good deal of learning and acumen. The account
given of *Taketori* mentions as sources of some of the elements
of the story the *Manyōshiu* and the *Kojiki*,[2] and among others
the Naigeden (內 外 典), whence a curious Buddhist legend
is cited to the following effect. Three recluses, after long-
continued meditation, found themselves possessed of the truth,
and so great was their joy that their hearts broke and they
died. Their souls thereupon took the form of bamboos with
leaves of gold and roots of precious jade, and after a period
of ten months had elapsed, the stems of these bamboos split
open and disclosed each a beauteous boy. The three youths
sat on the ground under their bamboos, and after seven days'
meditation they, too, became possessed of the truth, whereupon their bodies assumed a golden hue and displayed the
marks of saintliness, while the bamboos disappeared and
were replaced by seven magnificent temples. The legend
is manifestly of Indian origin, and seems to have been first
quoted by Kûkai or Kōbō Daishi from a sutra intituled
Hōrokaku (寶 樓 閣). Of the authorship of the *Taketori*
nothing certain is said to be known, but it is doubtfully
ascribed to one Minamoto Jun, who is also believed by some
to have had a hand in the composition of the *Utsubo monogatari*,[3] and the *Ochikubo monogatari*, both of which are

---

[1] See Mayers, *op. cit.*, Nos. 559 and 647. Compare also the description of
Amida's Paradise in Prof. Max Müller's translation of the text of the *Sukhavati*
brought from Japan. Part II. Vol. XII. of this Journal.

[2] Kaguya, for instance, is the name of a princess who is mentioned in the
history of the Mikado Suinin (B.C. 70–A.D. 70), and one of her five lovers is, I
believe, called Ōtomo no Miyuki (see the third Quest).

[3] An account of this work will, I believe, be found in the American Cyclopædia,
from the pen of Mr. Satow.

noticed in the *Gunsho*. The *Sumiyoshi monogatari* is a
lengthy love-story, the plot turning mainly upon the craft
and cruelty of a step-mother: it is considered one of the
best of the series. An old writer, says the *Gunsho*, ascribes
the authorship to the heroine of the tale, who is said to have
written the whole story on a screen in a small room near the
north-eastern gate of the Palace, which was a favourite
rendezvous for lovers. More popular, perhaps, is another
of the series, the *Yamato monogatari*, a collection of tales
from which Mr. Chamberlain has taken his pretty story of
the Maiden of Unai. It seems to have been, in part at
all events, written by the Retired Mikado Kwanzan (A.D.
983-5), and the accepted editions contain nearly three
hundred 'uta' or quintains. It is specially recommended,
together with the *Ise monogatari* and the *Genji monogatari*
to the attention of those who desire to become proficient in
the art of composing 'uta' with elegance and rapidity, an
art held in high honour at the court of the early Mikados.
For an account of the *Genji* the reader is referred to
Mr. Suyematsu's translation. The authoress, the Princess
Murasaki Shikibu, was asked, says the *Gunsho*, to compose
a story in a more modern style than that of the earlier
romances such as the *Taketori*, and this she was able to do
after passing a moonlit night in meditation and prayer. She
repented towards the close of her life of the frivolities of her
youth, and made with her own hands six hundred copies of
the Hanniya Sutra in order to merit salvation. The *Izumi
Shikibu monogatari*, which is next described, contains the lady's
correspondence with her lover, the fourth son of the Mikado
Reizei. Among the remaining *monogatari* a few only can
be briefly mentioned here. The *Ima monogatari* is rather a
series of poet-biographies than a romance, but it narrates,
among other curious matters, a singular dream of one of
its personages that Murasaki Shikibu may, after all,
have gone down into Hell. The sixty volumes of the
Ima mukashi monogatari (so called from its beginning
with the time-honoured phrase *ima mukashi* 'once upon
a time') describe the habits and customs of Japan

and India, the wonders to be found in both countries, the examples and effects of good and bad conduct they afford, and the traditions concerning the Buddha current in them.

The *Akinoyonaga no monogatari* (A Long Autumn-night's Story) is of later date. It narrates the unlawful loves of the priest Keikai, who lived in the reign of Horikawa II. (A.D. 1222-34), and is characterized as extremely pathetic and interesting. The priest finally repented of his evil ways and founded the temple of Unkyō. The *Matsuho monogatari* is similar to the last in style and matter. The *Omina meshi monogatari*, or 'Girls' Stories,' is a series of narratives of celebrated women, containing many wise saws and exemplary instances of successful diligence. Of the remainder of the nineteen *monogatari* enumerated, some are collections of essays rather than stories, and are evidently compilations. Indeed, in the Hewer's tale we have the only pure fiction of the whole series—at least the story of the Lady Kaguya may justly be so regarded—absolutely free from every trace of grossness, which is more than can be said of the *monogatari* which succeeded it. The word-plays it contains are its only blemishes, and these are far less common than in the later romances, where almost every page bristles with them. Even the narrative of the fifth Quest is rather vulgar and trivial than coarse in matter or manner, and in the imaginative literature of Japan which it ushered into being, the *Taketori monogatari* remains to the present day unsurpassed, nay unequalled, in purity, simplicity, pathos, and unstrained quality of style.

Three editions of the *Taketori* are known to me. One in two volumes has been already mentioned. Another, also in two volumes, published in the period Temmei 1781-9, is enriched with interpretative notes, by Koyama Tadashi. But the edition I have used is the work of Tanaka Daishu, a native of the province of Owari, which appeared in the year 1829. It is in six volumes, the first being an introductory essay upon the story and its sources, the remaining five volumes containing the text, distributed in short portions, each followed by a commentary, in which obsolete expressions and customs are explained, and various readings are presented and discussed, often at great length, and always with considerable learning and critical power.   I have subjoined Daishu's text romanized in accordance with the system adopted by the Rōmaji-kai (Society for the Romanization of Japanese—a reform I was the first to advocate some twenty years ago).   It does not appear that the *Taketori* was printed before the middle of the last century, and the text has doubtless suffered considerably at the hands of the MS. copyists, whose labours have handed it down during a period of eight hundred years. The language of the text, the oldest prose of the Altaic races,[1] is almost wholly archaic Japanese (*Yamato kotoba*) ; but a few Chinese expressions occur in it.   Originally it was probably written, like the *Manyōshiu*, partly in syllabic partly in Chinese, character, and the rendering of the latter into *Yamato kotoba* has, doubtless, not been accurately preserved in all cases.   It is worthy of notice, as showing the extent to which Japan merged whatever indigenous civilization she possessed in the imported civilization of China, that the *Taketori* hardly contains a single reference to Shintō or to any primitive tradition or myth.   So at the present day we see modern Japan, discarding Chinese modes of life and thought, engaged in a strenuous endeavour, despite her geographical remoteness, to gain a place in the great family of Western nations.

It had been my intention to extend these somewhat superficial notes so as to include some criticism of the text and an adequate examination of the Chinese and Sinico-Indian sources whence the author of the *Taketori* drew most of his materials.   But I found my own library quite insufficient for the purpose, and with regard to researches of the kind I had in view, the doors of the great library in Bloomsbury are practically closed to those who do not command a much more abundant leisure than I am ever likely to enjoy.

---

[1] The *Kojiki*, *Nihongi*, etc. are written in a style which is a bad imitation of Chinese.

THE TEXT.

KAGUYA HIME NO OI-TACHI.

Ima wa mukashi Taketori no okina to iyeru mono arikeri. Shigeyama ni majirite take wo toritsutsu, yorozu no koto ni tsukaikeri; na wo ba Sanugi no Miyakko to namu iikeru. Sono take no naka ni moto hikaru take namu hito suji arikeri. Ayashigarite yorite miru ni, tsutsu no naka hikaritari. Sore wo mireba, san sun bakari naru hito ito utsukushiute itari. Okina iu yō:
"Ware asa goto yū goto ni miru take no naka ui owasuru nite shirinu [1] ko ni naritamōbeki hito nameri.'' To te, te ni uchi-irete, iye ye motte kinu, me no ōna [2] ni azukarite yashinawasu. Utsukushiki koto kagiri-nashi, ito osanakereba ko [3] ni irete yashinau.
Taketori no okina take toru ni kono ko wo mitsukete. nochi ni take toru ni fushi wo bedatete, yo goto ni kogane aru take wo mitsukuru koto kasanarinu. Kakute okina yōyō yutaka ni nari-yuku. Kono chigo yashinau hodo ni sugu-suguto ōkini nari-masaru. Mi tsuki bakari ni naru hodo ni yoki hodo naru hito ni narinureba kamiage nado tadashite [4] kami-age-sesase mo [5] gisu chō [6] no uchi yori idasazu. Itsuki-kashizuki yashinau hodo ni kono chigo no katachi kyōra [7] naru koto yo ni naku, ya no uchi wa kuraki tokoro naku, hikari-michitari. Okina kokochi ashiku kurushiki toki mo kono ko wo mireba kurushiki koto mo yaminu haradatashiki koto mo nagusamikeri. Okina take wo toru koto hisashiku nari; ikioi mō [8] no mono ni nari ni keri.
Kono ko ito ōki ni narinureba, na wo ba Mimuro Imube no Akita wo yobite tsukesasu Akita Nayotake no Kaguya Hime to tsuketsn. Kono hodo mi ka uchi-age-asobu yorozu no asobi wo zo shikeru, otoko ōna kirawazu yobi-tsudoyete ito kashikoku asobu.

TSUMA-GOI.

Sekai no onoko, ate naru mo iyashiki mo, ikade kono Kaguya Hime wo yeteshi gana, miteshi gana to, oto ni kiki medete madō.
Sono atari no kaki ni mo, iye no to ni mo. oru hito da ni tawayasuku mirumajiki mono wo, yoru wa yasuki i mo nezu, yami no yo ni idete mo ana wo kujiri, koko kashiko yori nozoki, kaima mi-madoi ayeri. saru toki yori namu yobai to wa iikeru. Hito no monoshi to mo senu tokoro ni madoi arikedomo, nani no shirushi arubeku mo miyezu, iye no hito domo ni mono wo da ni iwamu tote iikakaredomo koto to mo sezu. Atari wo hanarenu kimi-tachi yoru wo akashi hi wo kurasu hito ōkari. Oroka naru hito wa yō naki ariki wa yoshinakarikeri tote kozu nari ni keri. Sono naka ni nawo iikeru wa; irogonomi to iwaruru hito go niu omoi yamu toki naku yoru hiru kitari keru. Sono na, hitori wa Ishizukuri no miko, hitori wa Kura-mochi no miko, hitori wa Sadaijin Abe no Miushi Dainagon, hitori wa Ōtomo no Miyuki Chiunagon, hitori wa Iso no Kami no Marotada kono hitobito narikeri. Yo no naka ni ōkaru hito wo da ni sukoshi mo katachi yoshi to kikite wa mima-hoshiu suru hitobito narikereba, Kaguya Hime wo mimahoshiushite mono mo kuwazu omoitsutsu; kono iye ni yukite tatazumi arikikeredomo ka-i arubeku mo arazu, fumi wo kakite yaredomo kayeri-goto mo sezu, wabi-uta nado kakite yaredomo kaveshi mo sezu, ka-i nashi to omoyedomo, shimotsuki shiwasu no furi, kōri, minazuki no teri-hatataku ni mo sawarazu kikeri. Kono hitobito aru toki wa Taketori wo yobi-idete "musume wo ware ni tabe'' to fushi-ogami te wo suri

---

[1] *Shiru* sometimes, as here, means to exercise power, have rights over, etc.

[2] *omina, onna.*   [3] *hako* or *kago.*

[4] *Sa-u-shite* (左 右), *sōshite, sōsoku (sōzoki?).*

[5] 裴.   [6] 帳 *kichō.*   [7] *kesō.*

[8] 猛. Most editions omit the sentence beginning with *ikioi.*

notamayeba " Ono ga nasanu ko nareba kokoro ni mo shitagawazu namu aru " to
iite, tsuki hi wo sugusu. Kakareba kono hitobito iye ni kayerite mono wo
omoi inori oshi guwan [1] wo tate omoi yamemu to suredomo yamubeku mo arazu.
Saritomo tsui ni otoko awasezaramu ya wa to omoite, tanomi wo kaketari,
anagachi ni kokoro-zashi wo miye arite, kore wo mitsukete Okina Kaguya Hime
ni iu yō :
"Waga ko no hotoke henguye no hito to mōshinagara warawa ōkisa made
yashinaitatematsuru kokoro-zashi orokanarazu okina no mōsamu hito kiki-tamaiten
ya."
To iyeba, Kaguya Hime :
"Nanigoto wo ka notomawamu koto wo uketamawarazaramu, henguye no
mono nite haberikemu mi to mo shirazu, oya to koso omoi-tatematsure." To
iyeba, okina : " Ureshiku notamō mono gana ! " to iu : " okina toshi nanasoji ni
amarinu, kyō tomo asu to mo shirazu, kono yo no hito wa, otoko wa ōna ni ō koto
wo su ōna wa otoko ni ō koto wo su, sono nochi namu kado mo hiroku nari-haberu,
ikadeka saru koto nakute wa owashimasenu."
Kaguya Hime no iwaku :
" Najō, saru koto ka shihaberamu " to iyeba, " Henguye no hito to iu tomo,
ōna no mi-mochi tamayeri, Okina no aramu kagiri wa kōte [2] mo imazu [3] kari
namu kashi, kono hitobito no toshi tsuki wo hete kō nomi imashitsutsu, notamō
koto wo omoi-sadamete, hitori-bitori ni aitatematsuritamaine " to iyeba, Kaguya
Hime iwaku : " Yoku mo aranu katachi wo fukaki kokoro mo shirade, ada
kokoro tsukinaba, nochi kuyashiki koto mo arubeki wo to omō bakari nari, yo
no kashikoki hito naritomo, fukaki kokorozashi wo shirade wa aigatashi to namu
omō " to iu. Okina iwaku : " Omoi no gotoku mo notamō kana ! Somosomo
ikayō naru kokorozashi aramu hito ni ka awamu to obosu kabakari, kokorozashi
orokanaranu hito bito ni koso amere." Kaguya Hime no iwaku : " Nani bakari
no fukaki wo ka mimu to iwamu isasaka no koto nari. Hito no kokorozashi
hitoshi kannari, ikadeka naka ni otorimasari wa shiranu. Go nin bito no naka
ni yukashiki mono wo misetamayeramu ni on kokorozashi masaritari tote tsuko-
matsuramu, to sono owasuramu hito bito ni moshi tamaye " to iu, " Yoki koto
nari " to uketsu. Hi kururu hodo rei no atsmarinu hitobito, aruiwa fuye wo
fuke, aruiwa uta wo utai, aruiwa shōga [4] wo shi, aruiwa uso wo fuki, ōgi wo
narashi nado suru ni Okina idete iwaku : " Katajikenaku mo kitanagenaru
tokoro ni toshi tsuki wo hete mono shitamō koto kiwamaritaru kashikomari to
mōsu, Okina no inochi kyō asu to mo shiranu wo, kaku notamō, [5] 'kimidachi ni mo
yoku omoi sadamete tsukōmatsure to mōseba fukaki no kokoro wo shirade wa to
namu mōsu, sa mōsu mo kotowari nari, izure otori-masari owashimaseneba yukashiki mono misetamayeramu ni on kokorozashi no hodo miyubeshi, tsukōmatsuramu
koto wa sore ni namu sadamubeki ' to iu ; kore yoki koto nari, hito no urami mo
uramaji " to iyeba, go nin no hitobito mo " Yoki koto nari " to iyeba, Okina
irite iu [6] : " Kaguya Hime Ishizukuri no miko ni wa, Tenjiku ni Hotoke no mi
ishi no hachi to iu mono ari, sore wo torite tamaye to iu ; Kuramochi no miko
ni wa, Higashi no umi ni Hōrai to iu yama annari, sore ni shirogane wo ne to
shi, kogane wo kuki to shi, shiraki tama wo mi to shite tateru ki are, sore hito
yeda orite tamawaramu to iu ; ima hitori ni wa Morokoshi ni aru hinezumi no
kawagoromo wo tamaye ; Ōtomo no Dainagon ni wa, tatsu no kubi ni go shiki
ni hikaru tama ari, sore wo torite tamaye ; Iso no kami no Chiunagon ni wa,

---

[1] *negai.* The words from *omoi* to *suredomo* are omitted in other editions.
[2] i.e. *kakute.*
[3] Perhaps *imazu* is a form of *ima zo.*
[4] 唱 歌.
[5] The subject of *notamō* is the Lady Kaguya.
[6] This very complicated sentence is a good example of the loose style of composition common among Japanese writers. The whole passage is corrupt ; another
rendering is *to mōshi mo kotowari nari, izure mo otori masari owashimaseneba
mi kokorozashi no wa mitamōbeshi tsukōmatsuran koto wa sore ni namu sadamubeki
to iyeba.* . . .

tsubakarame no motaru koyasugai torite tamaye" to iu. Okina, "kataki kotodomo ni koso amere, kono kuni ni aru mono ni mo arazu, kaku kataki koto wo ba ika ni mōsan" to iu: Kaguya Hime, "nanika katakaramu" to iyeba, Okina tomare kakumare mosamu tote idete, "kaku namu kikoyuru yō ni misetamaye" to iyeba, mikotachi-kamudachibe[1] kikite, "Oiraka ni 'atari yori da ni na ariki so' to ya wa notamawanu" to iite, unjite mina kayerinu.

HOTOKE NO MIISHI NO HACHI.

Nawo kono onna mide wa, yo ni arumajiki kokochi noshikereba, Temujiku ni aru mono mo mote konu mono ka wa to omoi megurashite, Ishizukuri no Miko wa, kokoro no shitakumi aru hito nite, Temujiku ni futatsu to naki hachi wo hyaku sen man ri no hodo ikitaru to mo, ikadeka torubeki to omoite, Kaguya Hime no moto ni wa kyō namu Temujiku ye ishi no hachi tori ni makaru to kikasete, mi tose bakari hete, Yamato no kuni, Tōchi no kōri ni aru yamadera ni Binzuru no maye naru hachi no hitakuro ni susuzukitaru wo torite, nishiki no fukuro ni irite, tsukuri-hana no yeda ni tsukite, Kaguya Hime no iye ni motekite misekereba, Kaguya Hime ayashigarite miru ni, hachi no nakani fumi ari, hirogete mireba :
"Umi yama no | michi ni kokoro wo | tsukushi-hate : | mi ishi no hachi no | namida nagare wa !"
Kaguya Hime hikari ya aru to miru ni hotaru bakari no hikari da ni nashi.
"Oku tsuyu no | hikari wo da ni mo | yado-sumashi : | Ogura no yama nite | nani motomekemu !"
Tote kayeshi-idasu. Hachi wo kado ni sutete kono uta no kayeshi wo su :
'Shirayama ni | ayeba, hikari no | usuru ka to ? | hachi wo sutete mo | tano-maruru kana !'
To yomite-iretari. Kaguya Hime kayeshi mo sezu narinu. Mimi ni mo kiki-irezarikereba iiwazuraite kayerinu. Kano hachi wo sutete mata iikeru yori zo omonaki koto wo ba "Hachi wo sutsuru" to zo iikeru.

HŌRAI NO TAMA NO YEDA.

Kuramochi no miko wa, kokoro tabakari aru hito nite, ōyake ni wa, Tsukushi no kuni ni yuami ni makaramu tote, itoma mōshite Kaguya Hime no iye ni wa, tama no yeda tori ni namu makaru to iwasete, kudaritamō ni tsukōmatsurubeki hitobito mina Naniwa made okuri-shikeri.
Miko ito shinobite to notomawasete, hito mo amata ite owashimasezu, chikō tsukōmatsuru kagiri shite, idetamainu, mi okuri no hitobito mi-tatematsuri okurite kayerinu, owashimashinu to hito ni wa miyetamaite mitsu hi bakari arite kogi-kayeri tamainu.
Kanete koto mina ohosetarikereba, sono toki ichi no takumi[2] narikeru Uchi marora roku nin wo meshitorite, tawayasuku hito yori-kumajiki iye wo tsukurite, kama ye wo miye ni shikomete, takumi-ra wo iritamaitsutsu, miko mo onaji tokoro ni komoritamaite, shirasetamaitaru kagiri jiu-roku so wo kami ni kudo wo akete, tama no yeda wo tsukuritamō.
Kaguya Hime notamō yō ni tagawazu tsukuri-idetsu. Ito kashikoku tabakarite Naniwa ni misoka ni mote idenu, fune ni norite kayeriki ni keri to tono ni tsuge yarite ito itaku kurushigenaru sama shite i-tamayeri.
Mukaye ni ni hito ohoku mairitari, tama no yeda wo zo nagahitsu ni irete, mono ohoite mochite mairu. "Itsuka kikemu Kuramochi no miko wa udomuguye no hana mochite nobori tamayeri !" to nonoshirikeri.
Kore wo Kaguya Hime kikite, "Ware wa kono miko ni makenu-beshi !" to mune tsuburete omoikeri. Kakaru hodo ni, kado wo tatakite "Kuramochi no miko owashitari" to tsugu.

---

[1] The word be has a collective force. Compare Imibe, etc. Kamudachi is equivalent to kami- or kimi-tachi.
[2] Of ichi no takumi a variant is hitotsu no takara.

Tabi no on sugata nagara, owashimashitari to iyeba aitatematsuru miko notamawaku : "Inochi wo sutete, kano tama no yeda mote kitari" tote Kaguya Hime ni misetatematsuritamayo to iyeba, Okina mochite iritari ; kono tama no yeda ni fumi wo zo tsuketari keru :

"Itazura ni | mi wa nashitsu to mo, | tama no ye wo | taorade sara ni | kayerazaramashi !"

Kore wo mo aware to mite oru ni Taketori no Okina hashiri irite iwaku : "Kono miko ni moshitamaishi Hōrai no tama wo yeda wo hitotsu no tokoro mo ayashiki tokoro naku ayamatazu, mote owashimaseri, nani wo mochite ka to kaku mōsubeki ni arazu. Tabi no mi-sugata nagara ware on iye ye mo yori-tamawazushite owashimashitari, haya kono miko ni aitsukōmatsuri tamaye" to iu ni mono mo iwadzu, tsurazuye mo tsukite imijiku nagekashige ni omoitari.

Kono miko ima sara nani ka to iubekarazu to iu mama ni, yen ni hai-nobori tamainu. Okina kotowari ni omo, "Kono kuni ni miyenu tama no yeda nari, kono tabi wa ikadeka inaiinosamu, hito sama mo yoki hito ni owasu" ii-itari.

Kaguya Hime no iu yō ; "oya no notamō koto wo hitaburu ni inabimōsanu koto no ito hoshisa ni yegataki mono wo yukashi to wa moshitsuru wo kaku asamashiku mote kuru koto namu netaku omoi haberu" to iyedo nawo Okina wa neya no uchi shitsurai nado su. Okina miko ni mosu yo : "Ikanaru tokoro ni ka kono ki wa sōraikemu, ayashiku uruwashiku medetaki mono ni mo" to mōsu.

Miko kotayete notomawaku : "Saotodoshi no kisaragi no tō ka goro ni, Naniwa yori tune ni norite, umi naka ni yukamu kata mo shirazu oboyeshikado, omō koto narade yo no naka no iki nani ka wa semu to omoishikaba, tada munashiki kaze ni makasete ariku. Inochi shinaba, ikaga wa semu ; ikite aramu kagiri, kaku arikite Hōrai to iuramu yama ni au ya to umi ni kogi tadayoi-arikite, waga kuni no uchi wo hanarete ariki-makari shi ni, aru toki wa nami aretsutsu, umi no soko ni mo irinubeku ; aru toki ni wa, kaze ni tsukete shiranu kuni ni fuki-yoserarete, oni no yō naru mono idekite korosamu to shiki. Aru toki ni wa, koshi kata yuku suye mo shirade umi ni magiremu to shi, aru toki ni wa, kato tsukite, kusa no ne wo kuimono to shi, aru toki iwamu kata naku mukutsuge naru mono no kite kui-kakaramu to shiki, aru toki wa umi no kai wo torite inochi wo tsugu. Tabi no sora ni tasuko-tamōbeki hito mo naki tokoro ni iroiro no yamai wo shite yuku kata sora mo oboyezu, fune no yuku ni makaseto umi ni tadayoite iho ka to iu. Tatsu no koku bakari ni umi no naka ni wazuka ni yama miyu. Fune no uchi wo namu semete miru. Umi no uye ni tadayoeru yama ito ōki nite ari. Sono yama no sama takaku uruwashi. Kare ya waga motomuru yama naramu to omoite sasuga ni osoroshiku oboyete yama no meguri wo sashimegurashite futsu ka mi ka bakari mi-ariku ni, amabito no yosohoi shitaru ouna yama no naka yori idekite shiroganc no kanamaru wo mochite mizu wo kumiariku. Kore wo mite, fune yori orite, "Kono yama no na wo nani to ka mōsu" to tō. Ouna kotayete iu, "Kore wa Hōrai no yama nari" to kotau. Kore wo kiku ni, ureshiki koto kagiri nashi. "Kono ouna kaku notamō wa tazo" to tō. "Waga na wa Hokaururi" to iite, futo yama no naka ni irinu."

"Kono yama wo miru ni, sara ni, noboru-beki sama nashi. Sono yama no sobazura wo megureba, yo no naka ni naki huna no ki domo tateri, kogane, shirogane, ruri iro no mizu nagareidetaru. Sore ni wa iro-iro no tama no hashi wataseri, sono atari ni teri kagayaku ki-tomo tateri, sono naka ni kono torite mochite mōde kitarishi wa ito warokarishi ka domo, notamaishi ni tagawamashikaba tote, kono hana wo torite mōde kitaru nari. Yama wa kagiri-naku omoshiroshi, yo ni tatōbeki ni arazarishi ka do, kono yeda wo oriteshikaba, sara ni kokoromoto nakute, fune ni norite, oi-kaze fukite, shi hyaku yo nichi ni namu mōde-ki ni shi. Dai kuwan no chikara ni ya Naniwa yori kinō namu Miyako ni mōde kitsuru, sara ni shiwo ni nuretaru kinu wo da ni nugi-kayenade namu kochi mōde kitsuru" to notamayeba, Okina kikite, uchinagekite yomeru :

"Kuretake no | yoyo no taketoru | no yama ni mo, | saya wa wabishiki | fushi wo nomi miji !"

Kore wo miko kikite, kokora no higoro omoiwabi-haberitsuru kokoro wa, kyō namu ochi-inuru to notamaite kayeshiseshi :

"Waga tamoto | kiyō kawakereba, | wabishiki no | chigusa no kazu mo | wasurarenubeshi !"

4

To notamai ; kakaru hodo ni otokodomo roku nin tsuranete niwa ni idekitari ; hitori no otoko fubasami ni fumi wo hasamite mōsu :

" Tsuku mo dokoro no zukasa no takumi Ayabe no Uchimaro mōsaku : Tama no ki wo tsukuritsukōmatsurishi kokoro wo kudakite, sen yo nichi ni chikara wo tsukushitaru koto sukunakurazu, shikaru ni roku imada tamawarazu, kore wo tamawarite wakachite kego ni tamawasen " to iite sasugetaru.

Taketori no Okina kono takumira ga mōsu koto wa nanigoto zo to katabuki-ori, miko wa ware ni mo aranu kimo kiyenubeki kokochi shite itamayeri.

Kore wo Kaguya Hime kikite, kono tatematsuru fumi wo " tore " to iite mireba, fumi ni moshikeru yo " Miko no Kimi sen yo nichi iyashiki takumira to morotomo ni onaji tokoro ni kakure i-tamaite, kashikoki tama no yeda wo tsukurase-tamaite, tsukasa mo tamawamu to ose-tamaiki ; kore wo kono goro auzuru ni mi tsukai to owashimasubeki Kaguya Hime no yōji tamōbeki narikeri to uke tamawatte kono miya yori tamawaramu to mōshite tamawarubeki nari."

Kaguya Hime kururu mama ni omoi-wabitsuru kokochi yemi sakayete, Okina wo yobitorite iu yō : Makoto Hōrai no ki ka to koso omoitsure ! kaku asamashiki sora goto nite arikereba, haya tote kayeshi tamaye," to iyeba, Okina kotō : " sadaka ni tskurasetaru mono to kikitsureba, kayesamu koto ito yasushi to unazuki ori."

Kaguya Hime no kokoro yukihatete aritsuru uta no kayeshi :

" Makoto ka to | kikite mitsureba, | koto no ha wo | kazareru tama no | yeda ni zo arikeru ! "

To iite, tama no yeda mo kayeshitsu. Taketori no Okina sabakari kataraitsuru ga sasuga ni oboyete neburi ori. Miko wa tatsu mo hashita, iru mo hashita uite itamayeri hi no kurenureba suberi detamainu.

Kano ureyeseshi takumi ra wo ba, Kaguya Hime yobisuyete, ureshiki hito domo nari to iite, roku ito ōku torase-tamō ; takumira imijiku yorokobite " omoitsuru yō ni mo aru kana !" To iite, kayeru michi nite, Kuramochi no miko, chi no nagaruru made chōzesasetamō, roku yeshi kaï mo naku, mina torisutesasc tamaite kereba, nige-use ni keri.

Kakute kono miko isshō no haji, kore ni suguru wa araji, ouna wo yezu narinuru nomi ni arazu ; ame no shita no hito no omowamu koto no hazukashi koto to notamaite, tada hito tokoro fukaki yama ye iritamainu. Miya-zuknsa sōrō hito bito mina te wo wakachite motome-tatematsuredomo ou shini mo ya shitamaikemu ye-mi-tsuke-tatematsurazu narinu. Miko wa mi tomo ni da ni kakushi-tamawamu tote, toshi goro miyetamawazarikeru narikeri. Kore wo nanu tamazukaru to wa ii-hajimekeru.

HINEZUMI NO KAWAGOROMO.

Sadai-jin Abe no Miushi wa, takara yutaka ni iye hiroki hito ni zo owasbikeru. Sono toshi watarikeru Morokoshi fune no Wokei to iu mono no moto ni fumi wo kakite, Hinedzumi no Kawagoromo to iu naru mono kaite okoseyo tote, tsuko-matsuru hito no naka ni kokoro tashikanaru wo yerabite, Ono no Fusamori to iu hito wo tsukete tsukawasu.

Mote itarite kano ura ni oru Wokei ni kogane wo torasu. Wokei fumi wo hirogete mite kaberigoto kaku, " Hinedzumi no Kawagoromo waga kuni ni naki mono nari, oto ni wa kikedomo imada minu mono nari, yo ni aru mono naraba kono kuni ni mo mote mōdeki namashi ; ito kataki akinai nari ; shikaredomo moshi Temujiku ni tama-saka ni mote watarinaba, moshi chōja no atari ni toburai motomemu ni naki mono naraba tsukai ni soyete kogane wo ba kayeshi tatematsuramu " to iyeri.

Kano Morokoshi fune ki-keri Ono no Futamori mōde kite, mō noboru to iu koto wo kikite, ayumi-tō suru muma wo mote hashirase mukaye-sase-tamō, toki ni, muma ni norite, Tsukushi yori tada nanuka ni nobori-mōde kitari. Fumi wo miru ni iwaku " Hinedzumi no Kawagoromo karōjite, hito wo dashite motometo tatematsuru. Ima no yo ni mo, mukashi no yo ni mo, kono kawa wa tawayasuku naki mono narikeri. Mukashi kashikoki Temujiku no hijiri kono kuni ni moto watarite tsukamatsurikeri. Nishi no yama-dera ni ari to kiki-oyobite oyake ni mōshite karojite, kai-totte-tatematsuru, atai no kane sukunashi to kokushi tsukai ni mōshikaba, Wōkei ga mono kuwayete kaitari. Ima kogane gojiu riyō tamawarubeshi. Fune no kayeramu ni tsukete tabi-okure, moshi kano tamawanu mono naraba kano koromo wo shichi kayeshi tabe" to iyeru koto wo mite :

"Nani obosu, inna kogane sukoshi no koto ni koso anare, kanarazu okurubeki mono ni koso anare, ureshikushite okosetaru kana!" tote, Morokoshi no kata ni mukaite fushi-ogami-tamō. Kono kawa-goromo iretaru hako wo mireba kusa gusa no uruwashiki ruri wo iroyete tsukureri.

Kawagoromo wo mireba, konjō no iro nari, ke no suye ni wa kogane no terashi kagayaki-tari, ge ni takara to miye, uruwashiki koto narabubeki mononashi. Hi ni yakenu koto yori mo kiyōra naru koto narabi nashi. "Ube; Kaguya Hime no konomoshikaritamō ni koso arikere!" to notamaite "ana kashiko!" tote hako ni iretamaite, mono no yeda ni tsukete, on mi no keso itō itakushite, yagate tomari unmu mono zo to oboshite, uta yomi-kuwayete mochite imashitari: sono uta wa :

"Kagiri naki | omoi ni yakenu | Kawagoromo; | tamoto kawakite | kiyō koso wa mime" to iyeri.

Iye no kado ni mote itarite tateri, Taketori idekite tori-irite, Kaguya Hime ni misu. Kaguya Hime kano kawagoromo wo mite iwaku: "Uruwashiki kawa nameri, wakite makoto no kawa naran to mo shirazu." Taketori kotayete iwaku: "Tomare kakumare mazu shōji iretatematsuran yo naka ni miyenu kawagoromo no sama nareba, kore we makoto to omoi-tamaiue, hito na itaku wabi-sase-tamaizo" to iite yobi-suye-tatematsureri.

Kaku yobi-suyete kono tabi wa kanarazu awan to ōna no kokoro ni mo omoi ori; kono Okina wa Kaguya Hime no yamome naru wo nagekashi-kereba, yoki hito ni awasemu to omoi hakaredomo sechi ni ina to iu koto nareba yeshiinu wa kotowari nari.

Kaguya Hime Okina ni iu: "Kono kawagoromo wa hi ni yakamu ni yakezuba koso makoto narame to omoite, hito no iū koto ni mo makenn, yo ni naki mono nareba, kore wo makoto to utagai naku omowan to notamō, nawo kore wo yakite kokoromite" to iu. Okina, "sore sa mo iwaretari" to iite, Daijin ni kaku nanu mashi to iu; Daijin kotayete iu. "Kono kawa wa Morokoshi ni mo nakarikeru wo karōjito motometazuue yetaru nari; nani wo utagai aramu, sa wa mōsu to mo haya yakite mitamaye" to iyeba, hi no naka in uchikubete yakasetamō ni, mera-mera to yakenu. Sareba koso koto-mono no kawa nari keri to iū.

Daijin kore wo mi-tamaite, on kao wa kusa no ha no iro nite i-tamayeri. Kaguya Hime wa, "Ana ureshi!" to yorokobite itari. Kano yomi-tamaikeru uta no henji hako ni irete kayesu :

"Nagori naku mo | moyu to shiriseba, | Kawagoromo. | Omoi no hoka ni | okite mimashi wo." | to arikeru, sareba kayeri imashi ni keri.

Yo no hito-bito "Abe no Daijin Kinedzumi no Kawagoromo wo mote imashite, Kaguya Hime ni sumitamō to na koko ni ya imasu?" nado to, aru hito no iu: "Kawa wa hi ni kubete yakitarishikaba mera mera-to yake ni shikaba Kaguya Hime aitamawazu" to ii-kereba, kore wo kiito zo togenaki mono wo ba "abenashi" to iikeru.

TATSU NO KUBI NO TAMA.

Ōtomo no Miyuki no Dainagon wa, waga iye ni ari to aru hito wo atsumete, notamawaku, "Tatsu no kubi ni go shiki no hikari aru tama anari, sore wo torite tatematsurituramu hito ni wa negawamu koto wo kanawamu" to notamō. Onoko tomo ōse no koto wo kikite mōsaku: "Owase no koto wa itomo tōtoshi, tadashi kono tama tawayasuku yuki-torashi wo, iwanya! Tatsu no kubi no tama wa ikaga toramu" to mōshi ageri. Dainagon notamō: "Kimi no tsukai to iwan mono wa, inochi wo sutete mo one ga kimi no ōse koto woba kanawamu to koso omōbekere. Kono kuni ni naki, Temujiku, Morokoshi no mono ni mo arazu. Kono kuni no umi yama yori tatsu wa ori notoru mono nari; ikani omoite ka, nanjira kataki mono to mosuheki?" Onoko tomo mōsu yo: "Saraba, ikaga wa sen, kataki mono nari tomo, ōseru ni shitagate, motome ni makaramu" to mōsu ni Dainagon miwaraite. "nanjira ya kimi no na wo nagashitsu kimi no ōse koto wo zo ikaga somukubeki?" to notamō.

Tatsu no kubi no tama tori ni tote idashite tamō. Kono hito bito no michi no kate kui mono ni tono no uchi no kinu, wata, zeni nado, aru kagiri tori idesoyete tsukawasu. Kono hito bito tomo kayeru made, imoi wo shite, ware wa oramu, kono tama toreyede wa mayc ni kayerikuna to notamawasekeri. Ono ono ōse uketamawarite makari-idenu.

"Tatsu no kubi no tama toriyezuba kayerikuna!" to notamayeba, izuchi mo, izuchi mo, ashi no mukitaramu kata ye inan to su; kakaru suki goto wo shitamō koto to soshiri ayeri tamawasetaru mono wa, ono ono wake tsutsu tori, aruiwa ono ga iye ni komori-i aruiwa ono ga yukamahoshiki tokoro ye inu.

Oya kimi to mosu tomo, kaku tsukinaki koto wo ōse tamō koto to koto yukanu mono yuye Dainagon wo soshiri-aitari.

Kaguya Hime suyemu ni wa rei no yō ni wa mi-nikushi to notamaite, uruwashiki ya wo tsukuritamaite, urushi wo nuri, makiye wo shi iroyeshi-tamaite, ya no uye ni wa, ito wo somete iro iro ni fukasete, uchi uchi no shitsurai ni wa iubeku mo aranu; aya orimono ni ye wo kakite magoto ni haritari.

Moto no medomo wa mina oi-haraite Kaguya Hime wo kanarazu awamu mōkeshite, hitori akashi kurashi tamō. Tsukawashishi bito wa, yoru hiru machi tamō ni, toshi koyuru made, oto mo sezu. Kokoromoto nagarite, ito shinobite, tada toneri futabito meshitsugi to shite, yatsuretamaite, Naniwa ni owashima-shite, toitamō koto wa, "Ōtomo no Dainagon no hito ya, fune ni norite, tatsu koroshite, so ga kubi no tama toreru to ya kiku" to towasuru ni, funabito kotayete iwaku: "Ayashiki koto kana!" to warnite, "Saru[1] waza suru fune mo nashi!" to kotayuru ni, "Ojinaki koto suru funabito ni mo aru kana! yeshirade kaku iu to oboshite, waga yumi no chikara wa tatsu araba futo i-koroshite, kubi no tama wa toritemu, osoku kuru yatsubara wo mataji" to notamaite, fune ni norite, umi koto ni ariki-tamō ni, ito tohokute Tsukushi no kata no umi kogi-ide-tamainu. Ikaga shikemu, hayaki kaze fukite, sekai kuragarite, fune wo fuki-mote ariku. Izure no kata tomo shirazu. Fune wo umi naka ni makari idenubeku; fuki-mawashite, nami wa fune ni uchikake-tsutsu maki-ire, nami wa ochi kakaru yō ni hirameki; kakuru ni Dainagon wa madoite, "mada kakaru wabishikime wa mizu, ikanaramu to suru zo!" to notamō, kajitori kotayete mōsu: "kokora fune ni norite makari ariku ni mada kaku wabishikime wo mizu, fune umi no soko ni irazuba, kami ochikakarinubeshi, moshi saiwai ni kami no tasuke araba, nankai ni fukare-owashinubeshi, utate aru nushi no on moto ni tsukayematsurite, susuro naru shini wo subekameru kana" to kajitori naku.

Dainagon kore wo kikite, notamawaku, "Fune ni norite wa, kajitori no mōsu koto wo koso takaki yama to mo tanome nado, kaku tanomoshige-naki koto wo mōsu zo!" to awohedo wo tsukite, notamō.

Kaji tori kotayete mōsu: "Kami naraneba ani waza wo ka tsukōmatsuramu, kaze fuki nami hageshikeredomo kami saye itadaki ni ochikakaru yō naru wa tatsu wo korosamu to motometamai sōrayaba kaku annari; hayate mo tatsu no fukasuru nari, haya kami ni inori tamaye!" to iu.

"Yoki koto nari" tote, kajitori no mi kami kikoshimese, "Ojinaku, kokoro osanaku, tatsu wo korosamu to omoikeri, ima yori nochi wa ke no suye hito suji wo da ni ugokashi tsulamatsuraji" to yogoto wo hanachite, tachi-i naku naku, yobai-tamō koto, chitabi bakari moshitamō; ge ni ya aramu! yōyō kaminari yaminu, sukoshi akarite kaze wa nawo bayaku fuku Kajitori no iwaku; "Kore wa tatsu no shiwaza ni koso arikere, kono fuku kaze wa yoki hō no kaze nari, ashiki kata no kaze ni wa airazu, yoki kata ni omomukite fuku nari" to iyedomo, Dainagon wa kore wo kiki-ire-tamawazu. Mika yoka fukite, fuki-kayeshi yose-tari, hama wo mireba, Harima no Akashi no hama narikeri. Dainagon nankai no hama ni fuki-yoseraretaru ni ya aramu to omoite, ikitsuki fushi-tamayeri, fune ni aru onokodomo kuni ni tsugetaraba, kuni no tsukasa mōde-toburō ni mo ye-oki-agari-tamawade, funa-zoko ni fushi-tamayeri. Matsu-hara ni mi mushiro

---

[1] i.e. *sa aru.*

shikite oroshi-tatematsuru, sono toki ni zo nankai ni arazarikeri to omoite, karōjite, okingari-tamayeru wo, mireba, kaze ito omoki hito nite hara ito fukuro, konata, kanata no me ni wa sumomo wo futatsu tsuketaru yō nari. Kore wo mitatematsurite zo kuni no tsukosa mo hohoyemitaru. Kuni ni ōsetamaite, tagoshi tsukurasetamaite, nyōnyō ni nawarete, iye ni iritamainuru wo, ikadeka kikemu, tsukawashite, onoko domo mairite mōsu yō, "tatsu no kubi no tama wo yetorazorishikaba, namu, tono ye mo yemairazarishi, tama no torikatakarishi koto wo shiritamayereba, namu, kandō araji tote, mairitsuru" to mōsu. Dainagon oki-idete notamawaku "Namujira yoku mote kozu nariuu. Tatsu wa naru kami no mi nite koso arikere, sorega tama wo toramu tote, sokora no hitobito no gai serarenamu to shikeri, mashite, tatsu wo torayetaramashikaba, mata koto mo naku, iye wa gai serarenamashi, yoku torayezu nari ni keri. Kaguya Hime chō ō nusubito no yatsu ga hito wo korosamu to saru narikeri, ware no atari da ni ima wa tōraji, onokodomo mo na ariki so" tote, ware ni sukoshi nokoritarikeru monodomo wa, tatsu no tama toranu monodomo ni tabitsu. Kore wo kikite hanaretamaishi moto no uyo wa, hara wo kirite warnitamō, ito wo fukasete tsukurishi yane wa tobi-karasu no su ni mina kui-mote i ni keri. Sekai no hito no iikeru wa, Ōtomo no Dainagon wa, tatsu no kubi no tama ya torite owashitaru, ina sa mo arazu, on manako futatsu ni sumomo no yō naru tama wo zo soyete imashitaru, to iikereba, anata yegata! to iikeru yori zo, yo ni awanu koto wo ba Ana tayegata! to ii-hajimekeru.

TSUBAKURAME NO KOYASUGAI.

Chiunagon Isonokami Marotada wa iye ni tsukawaruru onoko tomo no moto ni "tsubakurame no su kuitaraba tsugeyo" to notamō wo uketamawarite : "Nani no yō ni ka aramu" to mōsu. Kotayete notamō yō : "Tsubakurame no niotaru koyasugai wo toramu riyō nari" to notamō. Onoko domo kotayete mōsu, "Tsubakurame wo amata koroshite miru ni da ni mo, hara ni naki mono nari ; tadashi ko umu toki namu ikadeka idasuramu to mōsu hito da ni mireba usenu" to mōsu.

Mata hito no mōsu yō : "ōizukasa no ii kashiku ya no mune ni tsuku no ana goto ni tsubakurame wa su wo kui aru ; sore ni mame naramu onoko domo wo ite makarite, agura wo yuiagete ukagawasemu ni, sokora no tsubakurame ko umasaramu ya wa, sate, koso torashime tamawame" to mōsu.

Chiunagon yorokobitamaite "okashiki koto ni mo aru kana ! mottomo yeshirazarikeri, kiyō aru koto moshitari" to notamaite mame naru onokodomo nijiu nin bakari tsukawashite ananai ni age-suyeraretari. Dono yori tsukai hima naku tamawasete koyasu no gai toritaru ka to mukawasetamō. Tsubakurame no hito no amata nobori itaru ni, su ni noborikozu, kakaru yoshi go henji wo moshikereba, kiki-tamaite, ikaga subeki to oboshimeshi wazurō ni kano tsukasa no kuwan-nin Kuratsu-maro to mōsu okina mōsu yō : "Koyasugai toramu to oboshimesaba, tabakari mōsamu" tote, on maye ni mairitareba, Chiunagon hitai wo awasete, mukai-tamayeri. Kuratsu Maro ga mōsu yō : "Kono tsubakurame koyasugai wa ashiku tabakarite torase-tamō nari ; sate wa, yetorasetamawaji, ananai ni odoro-odoro-shiku nijiunin no hito no nobotte habereba arete yori-mōde kozu namu. Sesasetamōbeki yō wa, kono ananai wo kobochite, hito mina shirizokite, mame nasamu hito hitori wo arako ni nosesu-shite, tsuna wo kamayete, tori no ko umamu ma ni tsuna wo tsuri-age-sasete futo koyasugai wo torasetamawamu namu yokarubeki" to mōsu. Chiunagon notamō yō : "Ito yoki koto nari" tote, ananai wo kobochite, hito mina kayeri mōdekinu. Chiunagon Kuratsu Maro ni notamawaku : "Tsubakurame wa, ikanaru toki ni ka ko wo umu to shirite hito wo ba agubeki" to notamō, Kuratsu Maro mōsu yō : Tsubakurame ko umamu to suru toki wa, o wo sasagete, nanatabi megurite, namu, umi otosumeru, sate, nanatabi meguramu ori hikiagete, sono ori koyasugai wa torasetamaye" to mōsu. Chiunagon yorokobitamaite yorozu no hito ni mo shirasetamawade, misoka ni tsukasa ni imashite, onokodomo no naka ni majirite, yoru wo hiru ni nashite, torashime tamō.

Kuratsu Maro kaku mōsu wo ito itaku yorokobitamaite notamō : "Koko ni tsukawaruru hito ni mo naki ni negai wo kanōru koto no ureshisa !" to iite, on zo nugite, kazuke-tamaitsu ; sara ni yosari kono tsukasa ni mōde-koto notamaite tsukawashitsu. Higurenureba kano tsukasa ni owashite mi-tamō ni, makoto ni tsubakurame su tsukureri, Kuratsu Maro ga mōsu yō o wo sasagete meguru ni, arako ni hito wo nosete, tsuriagesaocte, tsubakurame no su ni te wo sashiiresasete, saguru ni mono mo nashi to mōsu ni Chiunagon ashiku sagureba naki nari to haradachite, "Tare bakari oboyemu ni tote ware nobotte saguran" to notamaite, ko ni norite tsurare-noborite, ukagaitamayeru ni, tsubakurame o wo sasagete itaku meguru ni awasete, te wo sasagete saguritamō ni, te ni hirameru mono sawaru, toki ni "ware mono nigiritari ima wa oroshite yo, okina shiyetari !" to notamaite, atsumarite, toku orosamu tote, tsuna wo hiki sugishite, tsuna tayuru, sunahachi ni Yashima no kanaye no uye ni nokesama ni ochitamayeri.

Hito-bito asamashigarite, yotte, kakayetsukamatsureri, on me wa shirame nite fushi tamayeri, hitobito on kuchi ni mīzu wo sukui, iretsukamatsuru, karōjite iki detamayeru ni, mata kanaye no uye yori tetori, ashitori shite, sageoroshitatematsuru.

Karōjite, on kokochi wa ikaga obosaruru to toyaba, iki no shita nite mono wa sukoshi oboyuredo, koshi namu ugokarenu.

Saredo koyasugai wo futo nigiri motareba, ureshiku oboyuru nari. Mazu shisokuseshite, kokono kai gao mimu to tsukushi motagete on te wo hiroge tamayeru ni, tsubakurame no mariokeru furu kuso wo nigiritamayeru narikeri. Sore wo mitamaite, "ana! kaina no waza ya" to notamaikeru yori zo omō ni tagō koto wo zo "kai nashi" to iikeri.

Kai ni mo arazu to mitamaikeru ni, on kokochi mo tagaite, karabitsu no futa ni irare tamōbeku mo arazu. On koshi wa ore ni keri, Chiunagon wa iwaketaru waza shite yamu koto wo hito ni kikaseji to shitamaikeredo, sore wo yamai nite ito yowaku naritamai ni keri. Kai wo yetorazu narinikeru yori mo hito no kikiwarawamu koto wo hi ni soyete omoitamaikereba, tada ni yamishinuru yori mo hitogiki hazukashiku oboyetamō nari keri. Kore wo Kaguya Hime kikite tōrai ni tsukawashikeru uta:

"Toki wo hete, | nami tachi yaranu | Suminoye no | matsu kai nashi to | kiku wa makoto ka ?"

To aru wo yonde kikasu. Ito yowaki kokochi ni kashira motagete hito ni kami wo motasete kurushiki kokochi ni karōjite kakitamō:

"Kai wa kaku | arikeru mono wo | wabi-sutete, | shinuru inochi wo | sukui ya wa senu !"

To kaki hatsuru to taye-iri-tamainu. Kore wo kikite, Kaguya Hime, sukoshi aware to oboshikeri. Sore yori, namu, sukoshi ureshiki koto wo ba "kai ari" to zo iikeru.

MIKARI NO MIYUKI.

Sate Kaguya Hime katachi no yo ni nizu medetaki koto wo Mikado kikoshimeshite, naishi Nakatomi no Fusako ni notamō, "ōku no hito no mi wo itazura ni nashite awazanaru Kaguya Hime wa, ika bakari no ouna zo to makarite mite maire," to notamō. Fusako uketamawarite makareri, Taketori no iye ni kashikomarite shōji irite ayeri, ouna ni naishi notamo, "ōse goto ni Kaguya Hime no katachi iu ni oyobazu to nari, yoku mite mairubeki yoshi notamawaretsuru ni namu mairitsuru" to iyeba, "saraba kaku to mōshi-haberamu" to iite irinu.

Kaguya Hime ni, "Haya kano mi tsukai ni taimen shi-tamaye" to iyeba, Kaguya Hime, "yoki katachi ni mo aranu, ikadeka miyubeki" to iyeba, "utate mo notamo kana! Mikado no mi tsukai wo ba ikadeka oroka ui semu" to iyeba Kaguya Hime no kotayeru vō, "Mikado no meshite notawawamu koto kashikoshi to mo omowazu "to iite, sara ni miyubeku mo arazu. Umeru ko no yō ni wa aredo ito kokoro hazukashige ni orosokanaru yō ui iikereba kokoro uo mama ni mo yesemezu.

Ouna naishi no moto ni kayeri idete, "kuchioshiku kono osanaki mono wa kowaku haberu mono nite, taimensumajiki to mōsu." Naishi, "Kanarazu mitatematsurite maire to ōsegoto arit-uru mono wo mitatematsurade wa, ikadeka kayeri mairamu, koku-wō no ōsegoto wo masa ni yo ni sumitamawamu hito no uketamawari tamawade wa arinamu ya iwareuu koto nashitamai yo !" to kotoba

hajishiku iikereba, kore wo kikite, mashite Kaguya Hime kikubeku mo arazu
" Kokuwō no ōsegoto wo somukaba, haya koroshitamaite yokashi " to iu. Kono
naishi kayeri-mairite kono yoshi wo sōsu. Mikado kikoshimeshite " ōku no hito
koroshitegeru kokoro zo kashi !" to notamawaite yami ni keredo nawo oboshimeshi owashimashite, " Kono ouna no tabakari ni ya makemu " to oboshimeshite
Takctori no Okina wo meshite ōsetamō " Nanji ga motte haberu Kaguya Hime
tsukamatsure, kaokatachi yoshi to kikoshimeshite mi tsukai wo tabishikado kai
naku miyezu nari ni keri, kaku taidaishiku ya wa narawasubeki ? " to Okina kashikomarite, go henji mōsu yō, " kono me no warawa wa, tayete miyazukaye tsuko-
matsurubeku mo arazu haberu wo mote, wazurai haberu ; saritomo makarite ōse
tamawamu " to sōsu. Kore wo kikoshimeshite, on idasetamō " Nado ka ! Okina
no te ni okoshitatetaramu mono wo kokoro ni makasezaramu, kono ouna moshi
tate matsuritaru mono naraba Okina ni kōburi wo nado ka tabasezaramu."
Okina yorokobite iye ni kayerite, Kaguya Hime ni katarō yō, " Kaku namu
Mikado no ōsetamayeru nawo ya wa tsukōmatsuri-tamawann " to iyeba Kaguya
Hime notamawaite iu, " mohara sayō no miyazukaye tsukōmatsuraji to omō wo
shiite tsukōmatsurase-tamawaba kiyeuse nari, mi zukasa kōburi-tskōmatsurite
shinu bakari nari." Okina irayuru yō, " Na shitamai zo, tsukasa kōburi mo
waga ko wo mitatematsurade wa, nani ni ka wa semu, sa wa aritomo nadoka
miyazukaye wo shitamawazaramu shinitamō-beki yō ya wa arubeki " to iu.
" Nawo sora goto ka to, tsukōmatsurasete shinazu ya aru to mite tamaye,
amata no hito no kokorozashi oroka-narazarishi wo munashiku nashite shi koso
are. Kinō kiyō Mikado no notamawamu koto ni tsukamu hitogiki yasashi " to
iyeba, Okina irayube iwaku, " amenoshita no koto wa, to aritomo kakaritomo,
ou inochi no ayōsa koso ōki naru sawari nareba nawo tsukōmatsurumajiki koto
wo, mairite mosamu " tote mairite mōsu yō, " ōse no koto no kashikoki ni kano
warawa wo mairasemu tote, tsukōmatsureba miyazukaye ni dashitatenaba shinu.
beshi to mōsu. Miyakko Maro ga te ni umasetaru mono ni mo arazu, mashishi
yama nite mitsuketaru ; kakareba kokoro-base mo yo no hito ni nizu zo haberu "
to sō-sesasu. Mikado ōsetamawaku, " Miyakko Maro ga iye wa yama moto
chikaku nari, mikari no miyuki shitamawamu yō nite mitemu ya," to notama-
wasu. Miyakko Maro ga mōsu yō, " Ito yoki koto nari, nanika kokoro mo nakute
aramu ni futo mi-yuki shite go ranzerare namu " to sōsureba Mikado niwaka ni
hi wo sadamete, mii kari ni ide tamaite, Kaguya Hime no iye ni iritamaite,
mii-tamō ni, hikari michite, kiyōra nite itaru hito ari, " kore naramu ! " to
oboshite chikaku yorasetamō ni nigete iru. Sode wo toraye-tamayeba, omote wo
futagite sorayedo, hajime yoku go rau-jitsureba, tagui-naku medetaku oboyesa-
setamaite, ' yurusaji to su' tote iteowashimasamu to suru ni, Kaguya Hime
kotayete sōsu, " onoga mi wa, kono kuni ni umarete haberaba, koso tsuka-
itamawame ; ito ite owoshimashigataku ya haberamu " to sōsu. Mikado,
nadoka sa aramu, nawo ite owashimasamu tote, on koshi wo yose-tamō ni
kono Kaguya Hime kito kago ni narinu ; hakanaku kuchi-oshi to oboshite, ge ni
tadabito ni wa arazarikeri to oboshite, " saraba, on moto ni wa ite-ikaji, moto
no on katachi ni nari-tamaine, sore wo mite da ni kayeri namu " to ōserareba,
Kaguya Hime moto no katachi ni narinu. Mikado nawo medetaku oboshi-
mesaruru koto sekitome-gatashi, kaku misetsuru Miyakko Maro wo yorokobi-
tamō ; sate, tsukamatsuru hiyaku-kuwan hitobito ni aruji ikameshiu tsukōmatsuru.
Mikado Kaguya Hime wo todomete kayeri-tamawamu koto wo akazu kuchioshiku oboshikeredo, tamashii wo todometaru kokochi shite, namu, kayera-
setamaikeru on koshi ni tatematsurite, nochi ni Kaguya Hime ni :
" Kayeru sa no | myuki mono uku | omohoyete; | somukite tomaru | Kaguya
Hime yuye ! "
Go henji wo :
" Mugura hafu | shimo ni mo toshi wa | henuru mi no | nanika wa tama no |
utena wo mo mimu."
Kore wo Mikado goranjite, itodo kayeritamawamu, sora mo naku obosaru, mi
kokoro wa sara ni tachi-kayerubeku mo obosarezarikeredo, saritote, ya wo
akashitamōbeki ni mo araneba kayerasetamainu.
Tsune ni tsukōmatsuru hito wo mitamō ni Kaguya Hime no katawara ni

yorubeku da ni arazari keri, koto hito yori wa kiyōra nari to oboshikeru hito, kare ni oboshi-awasureba hito ni mo arazu.   Kaguya Hime nomi on kokoro ni kakarite tada hitori sugushitamō, yoshinakute on katagata ni mo wataritamawazu. Kaguya Hime no moto ni zo mi fumi wo kakite kayowasase tamō, go henji sasuga ni nikukarazu kikoyekawashitamaite, omoshiroki ki-gusa ni tsukete mo, on uta wo yomite tsukawasu.

AMA NO HAGOROMO.

Kayō nite on kokoro wo tagai ni nagusame tamō hodo ni mi tose bakari arite, haru no hajime yori Kaguya Hime tsuki no omoshirō idetaru wo mite, tsune yori mo mono omoitaru sama nari.   " Aru hito no tsuki no kawo miru wa, imu koto!" to seishikeredomo, tomo sureba hito-ma ni mo tsuki wo mite wa imijiku naki-tamō.   Fu-tsuki no mochi no tsuki ni ide-ite, sechi ni mono omoyeru keshiki nari.   Chikaku tsukawaruru hitobito Taketori no Okina ni tsugete iwaku, " Kaguya Hime rei mo tsuki wo aware gari-tamai keredo, kono goro to narite wa tada-koto ni mo haberazameri, imijiku oboshinageku koto arubeshi yoku yoku mi-tsukamatsurase-tamaye " to iu wo kikite, Kaguya Hime ni iu yō: " najō kokochi sureba, kaku mono wo omoitaru sama nite, tsuki wo mitamō zo, umashiki yo ni " to iu.   Kaguya Hime "tsuki wo mireba, yo no naka kokoro-bosoku aware ni haberi najō mono wo ka nageki ni haberu beki " to iu.   Kaguya Hime no aru tokoro ni itari mireba nawo mono omoyeru keshiki nari.   Kore wo mite, "aga hotoke! nani goto omoitamō zo? obosuramu koto nani goto zo?" to iyeba, "omō koto mo nashi mono, namu, kokoro-bosoku oboyuru" to iyeba, Okina, "tsuki na mi tamō zo. Kore wo mi-tamayeba mono obosu keshiki wa aru zo!" to iyeba, "ikade tsuki wo ba mizute wa aramu?" tote, nawo tsuki izureba ide-i-tsutsu, nageki omoyeri, yuyami ni wa mono omawanu keshiki nari.

Tsuki no hodo ni narinureba, nawo toki-doki wa uchinageki naki nado su. Kore wo tsukau monodomo nawo mono obosu koto arubeshi to sasayakedo, oya wo hajimete nanigoto to mo shirazu.

Hatsuki no mochi bakari no tsuki ni ideite Kaguya Hime ito itaku naki tamō, hito me mo ima wa tsutsumitamawazu naki tamō.   Kore wo mite, oyadomo mo "nani goto zo" toi-sawagu.   Kaguya Hime naku naku iu "Saki-zaki ino mōsamu to omoishikadomo, kanarazu kokoro madowashitamawamu mono zo to omoite, ima made sugushi haberitsuru nari.   Sa nomi ya wa tote, uchi-ide haberinuru zo onoga mi wa kono kuni no hito ni mo arazu, tsuki no miyako no hito nari.   Sore wo mukashi no chigiri arikeru ni yorite namu kono sekai ni wa mōdekitarikeru, ima wa kayerubeki ni ki ni kereba, kono tsuki no mochi-hi ni kano moto no kuni yori mukaye ni hitobito mōde komuzu sarazu makarinubekereba, oboshi nagekamu ga kanashiki koto wo kono haru yori omoi-nageki haberu nari " to iite imijiu naku. Okina wa, "najō koto wo notamō zo? take no naka yori mitsuke kikoyetarishikado natane no ōkisa owaseshi wo waga take-dachi narabu made yashinai-tatematsuri-taru, waga ko wo nani bito ga mukaye kikoyemu.   Masa ni yurusamu ya " to iite, ware koso shiname tote naki-nonoshiru koto ito tayegatage nari.

Kaguya Hime no iwaku, "Tsuki no miyako no hito nite, chichi haha ari; kata toki no ma tote kono kuni yori mōde-koshikadomo, kaku kouo kuui ni wa amata no toshi wo henuru ni namu arikeru.   Kano kuni no chichi haha no koto mo oboyezu, koko ni wa kaku hisashiku asobi-kikoyete narai-tatematsureri, imijikaramu kokochi mo sezu kanashiku nomi, namu, aru.   Saredo ono ga kokoro narazu makari namu to suru " to iite morotomo ni imijiu naku.

Tsukawaruru hito bito mo toshigoro naraite, tachiwakare, namu, koto wo kokorobaye nado ateyaka ni utsukushikaritsuru koto wo minaruite, koishikaramu koto no tayegataku, yumizu mo nomarezu onaji kokoro ni nagekashigarikeri.

Kono koto wo Mikado kikoshimeshite Taketori no iye ni on tsukai tsukawasa-setamō.   On tsukai ni Taketori ideaite naku koto kagiri-nashi.   Kouo koto wo nageku ni, hige mo shiroku, koshi mo kagawari, me mo tadare ni keri.   Okina kotoshi wa isoji bakari narikeredo, mono omoi ni wa kata toki ni namu oi ni nari ni keri to miyu.

On tsukai ōsegoto tote Okina ni iwaku, "Ito kokorogurushiku mono omō naru wa makoto ni ka to ōsetamō?"   Taketori nakunaku mōsu, "kono mochi ni, namu, tsuki no yori Kaguya Hime no mukaye ni mōdeku naru; tōtoku towase-

tamō kono mochi ni wa hitobito tamawarite tsuki no miyako no hito mōde koba
toraye-sasemu" to mōsu.

On tsukai kayerimairite, Okina no arisama mōshite sōshi-tsuru koto domo
mōsu wo kikoshimeshite notamō, "Hito me miitamaishi mi kokoro ni da ni
wasuretamawanu ni, akegure minaretaru Kaguya Hime wo yarite wa ikaga
omōbeki!" Kano mochi no hi tsukasa-zukasa ni ōsete chokushi ni wa, shōshō
Takano no Ōkuni to iu hito wo sashite rokuye no tsukasa awasete ni sen nin no
hito wo Taketori no iye ni tsukawasu.

Iye ni makarite tsui-hi-ji no uye ni sen nin, ya no uye ni sen nin, iye no hitobito ito ōkurikeru ui, awasete, akeru hima mo naku mamorasu. Kono mamoru
hitobito mo yumi ya wo taishite ori, moya no uchi ni wa, ouna domo wo ban ni
suyete mamorasu. Ouna nuri-gome no uchi ni Kaguya Hime wo idakayete ori,
Okina mo nurigome no to wo sashite tokuchi ni ori; Okina no iu "kabakari
mamoru tokoro ni ama no hito ni mo makemu ya "to iite, ya no uye ni oru
hitobito ni iwaku, "Tsuyu mo mono sora ni kakeraba futoi-koroshitam uye!"
Mamoru hitobito no iu "Kabakarishite mamoru tokoro ni kabahori hitotsu da ni
araba mazu i-koroshite to ui sarasamu to omoihaberu "to iu; Okina kore wo
kikite tanomoshigari ori.

Kore wo kikite, Kaguya Hime wa, "Sashikomete, mamori tatakaubeki shitakumi wo shitaritomo, ano kuni no hito wo yetatakawanu nari; yumiya shite
irareji, kaku sushikomete aru tomo kono kuni no hito koba mina akinamu to su,
aitatakawamu to su tomo kano kuni no hito kinaba takeki kokoro tsukau hito mo
yō mo araji." Okina no iu yō "on mukayeni komu hito wo ba, nagaki tsume shite,
manako wo tsukami-tsubasamu, sakagami wo torite, kanaguri otosamu, sagashiri
no kaki-idete-kokoro no ōyake hito ni misete haji misemu" to hara-dachi oru.

Kaguya Hime iwaku, ukowa-daka ni na notamai zo, ya no uye ni oru hitodomo
no kiku ni ito masanashi. Ima sukarizuru kokorozashi domo wo omoi mo
shirade-makari namu zuru koto no kuchioshiu habekeri, nagaki chigiri no
nakari-kereba, hodonaku makarinubeki nameri to omōga kanashiku haberu nari.
Oya tachi no kayeri-mi wo isasaka da ni tsukematsurade makaramu michi mo
yasuku mo arumajiki ni tsuki goro mo idete, kotoshi bakari no itoma wo moshi-
tsuredo, sara ni yurusarenu ni yotte, namu, kaku omoi nageki haberu on kokoro
wo nomi madowashite sari namu koto no kanashiku tayegataku haberu nari. Kano
miyako no hito wa ito kiyōra nite oi mo sezu, namu, omō koto mo naku haberu
nari. Saru tokoro ye makaramuzuru mo imijiku mo haberazu. Oi otoroye
tamayeru sama wo mi tatematsurazaramu koso koishikarame" to iite naku.

Okina mune idaki," koto na shi tamō zo, urawashiki sugata shitaru tsukai ni
mo sawaraji "to notami ori. Kakaru hodo ni yohi uchisugite ne no toki
bakari ni, iye no atari, hiru no akasa ni mo sugite, hikaritari, mochi-tsuki no
akasa wo to wo awasetaru bakari nite, aru hito no ke no ana saye miyuru hodo nari.

O-zora yori hito kumo ni uorite, orikite, tsuchi yori go shaku bakari agaritaru
hodo ui tachitsuraretari; kore wo mite uchi soto naru hito no kokoro tomo mono
ni osowaruru yō nite aitatakawamu kokoro mo nakarikeri, karōjite, omoi okoshite,
yumi ya toritatemu to suredomo, te ni chikara mo nakunarite nayekagamaritaru
naka ni kokoro sakashiki mono nenjite in to suredomo, hoka zama ye kikereba
are mo tatakawade, kokochi tada shire ui shirete mamori ayeri.

Tateru hito-domo wa, sōzoku no kiyūra naru koto mono ni mo nizu, tobu
kuruma hitotsu gushitari, rakai sashitari, sono naka ni wō to oboshiki hito
iye ni" Miyakko Maro mōde-ko! "to iu ni, takeku omoitsuru Miyakko Maro mo
mono ni yeitaru kokochi shite, utsubushi ni fuseri. Iwaku," nanji osanaki hito,
isasaka naru kudoku wo Okina tsukurikeru ni yorite, nanji ga taske ni tote, kata-
koki no hodo tote, kudashishi wo, sokora no toshigoro, sokora no kogane tamaito,
mi wo kayetaru ga gotoku nari ni keri. Kaguya Hime wa tsumi wo tsukuri tamayeri
kereba, kaku iyashiki onore ga moto ni shibashi owashitsuru nari; tsumi no kagiri
hate-nureba, kaku mukōru wo Okina wa naki nageku atawanu koto nari, haya
kayeshi tatematsure" to iu. Okina kotayete mōsu; "Kaguya Hime wo yashinaitatematsuru koto hata tose amari ni narinu. Kata-toki to notamo ni ayashiku nari
haberinu, mata koto tokoro ni Kaguya Hime to mōsu hito zo owashimasuramu" to
iu "koko ni owasuru Kaguya Hime wa omoki wazurai wo shitamayeba ye-ide
owashimasumaji" to mōseba, sono henji wa nakute ya no uye ni tobu kuruma wo

yosete "iza Kaguya Hime kitanaki tokoro ni ikadeka hisashiku owasemu" to ii-tate kometaru tokoro no to sunawachi tada aki ni akinu kōshidomo, mo hito wa nakushite akinu, ouna idakite, Kaguya Hime to ni idenu, ye-todomumaji-kereba, tada sashi-ōgite naki ori. Taketori kokoro madoite naki-fuseru tokoro ni yorite Kaguya Hime iu, "Koko ni mo, kokoro ni mo arade, kaku makaru ni noboramu wo da ni, mi-okuri tamaye" to iyedomo "nani shi ni kanashiki ni mi-okuri tatematsuramu, ware wo ika ni se³⁰ tote, sutete wa, nohori tamō zo gu-shite ite owasene" to nakite fusereba, on kokoro madoinu, fumi wo kaki okite makaramu, koishikaramu ori-ori tori-dashite mi-tamaye, ..te uchi-nakite kaku kotoba wa, "kono kuni ni umarenuru to naraba, nagekase-tatematsuranu hodo made haberubeki wo haberade sugiwakarenuru koto, kayesugayesu ho i naku koso oboye-habere, nugi-oku kinu wo katami to mi-tamaye, tsuki no idetaramu yo wa mi-okose-tamaye mi-sute-tatema tsurite makaru sora yori mo ochinubeki kokochi su" to kaki-oku.

Amabito no naka ni motosetaru hako ari; ama no ha-goromo ireri, mata aru wa fushi no kusuri ireri. Hitori no amabito iu "Tsubo naru on kusuri tatema-tsure, kitanaki tokoro no mono kikoshimeshitareba on kokochi ashikaramu mono zo" tote, mote yoritareba, isasaka name-tamaite, sukoshi katami tote, nugi oku kinu ni tsutsumamu to sureba, aru amabito "tsutsumasezu" on zo wo tori-idashite kisemu to su.

Sono toki ni Kaguya Hime, "shibashi mate" to iite "kinu kisetsuru hito wa ko-koro koto ni naru nari" to iu, "Mono hito goto iiokubeki koto ari nari" to iite, fumi kaki; Amabito "ososhi to kokoro moto nagari-tamō" Kaguya Hime "mono shiranu koto na notamai zo" tote, imijiku shidzuka ni ōyake ni mi fumi tatematsuritamō, awatenu sama nari. "Kaku amata no hito wo tamaite, todomesase-tamaycdo yuru-sanu, mukaye-mōdekite tori-ide makarinureba kuchioshiku kanashiki koto miyazuka-ye tsukōmatsurazu narinuru mo, kaku wazurawashiki mi nite habereba, kokoro yezu oboshimeshitsuramedomo, kokoro tsuyoku uketamawarazu nari ni shi koto namege naru mono ni oboshimeshi todomerarenuru namu kokoro ni tomari haberinu tote.

"Ima wo tote | ama no hagoromo | kiru ori zo | kimi wo aware! to | omoi-idekeru."

Tote tsubo no kusuri soyete tō no chiushō wo yobiyosete tatematsurasu, chiushō ni amabito torite tsutau, chiushō toritsureba futo ama no hagoromo uchi-kisereri tsureba, Okina wo ito oshikanashi to oboshitsuru koto mo usenu.

Kono kinu kitsuru hito wa, mono omoi naku nari ni kereba, kuruma ni norite hiyaku nin bakari amabito gushite noborinu. Sono nochi Okina ouna chi no namida wo nagashite madoyedo ka-i nashi. Ano kaki-okishi fumi wo yomite, kikase keredo "Nani semu ni ka, inochi mo oshikaramu taga tame ni ka, nanigoto mo yō mo nashi!" tote, kusuri mo kuwazu, yagate oki mo agarazu yami-fuseri.

Chiushō hitobito hikigushite kayeri-mawarite, Kaguya Hime wo ye-tatakai-tomezu narinuru wo komagoma to sōsu. Kusuri no tsubo ni on fumi soyete mairasu. Hirogete goranjite itaku awaregarasetamaite, mono mo kikoshimeosezu, mi asobi nado mo nakarikeri. Daijin-Kami-dachibe wo meshite izure no yama ka ama ni chikaki to towase-tamō ni, aru hito sōsu "Suruga no kuni ni aru yama,[1] namu, kono miyako chikaku, ama mo chikaku haberu" sōsu: kore wo kikase-tamaite.

"Au koto mo
n⸱mida ni ukabu
waga mi ni wa ;
shinanu kusuri wa
nani ni ka wa semu!"

Kano tatematsurareru shinanu no kusuri no tsubo ni on fumi gushite mi zukaye ni tamawasu, chokushi ni wa. "Tsuki no Iwakasa to iu hito wo meshite, Suruga no kuni ni a-naru yama no itadaki ni mote-yukubeki yoshi" ōsetamō.

Mine nite subeki yō oshiyesasetamō, "on fumi fushi no kusuri no tsubo narabete, hi wo tsukete moyasubeki yoshi" ōsetamo. Sono yoshi uketamawaite, mononofu mo amata gushite yama ye noborikeru yori, namu, sono yama wo Fuji no yama to wa nazukeru. Sono keburi imada kumo no naka ye tachi-noboru to zo iitsutayetaru.

---

[1] Also *aru naru yama.*

Since the publication in the Journal of the Asiatic Society of the foregoing version, accompanied by the romanised text, I have carefully gone over the latter and now subjoin some further corrections and observations, followed by a brief sketch of the grammar of the text, an analysis of part of it, and notes on the remainder, together with a full vocabulary. The most serious difficulty of the modern tongue lies in the acquisition of the extraordinarily complicated script in which it is written, and of its double vocabulary. Neither of these obstacles beset the study of the older, and only to a slight extent that of the later *Monogatari*, while this division of Japanese literature is, on the whole, the best prose literature the Japanese mind has produced. The Hewer's Tale is, as I have shown, the prototype of the *monogatari*, and with the aids now offered its text may be easily and completely mastered by any one possessed of some leisure and patience. I shall not consider my labours vain if I should thus attain some success in my endeavour to render this attractive branch of the literature of Old Japan more accessible than heretofore to the Western student.

On a closer review of the text it appears more corrupt than I had at first imagined. Daishu gives reasons usually for his emendations, often very ingenious ones, and these emendations I have generally adopted. But they are far from giving us a perfect text, now probably irrecoverable. Nor is Daishu always consistent; he writes the future, for instance, sometimes with *mu*, sometimes with *n*, and he applies the honorifics *mi* and *on* after an uncertain fashion. *Mu* appears to be the more correct form; compare the forms in *me* and *meru*, which seem to be emphatic forms of *mu*; and *mi* ought to be employed only as an honorific of what may appertain to the Mikado or his dignity.

In the transliteration, which was an afterthought, and had to be prepared within narrow limits of time, various errors remain, none of which, however, are of any great importance. They are corrected in the following pages. One of the commonest is the dissociation of auxiliaries, such as *tamai, haberi*, etc., from their principal verbs. *Dzu* is sometimes printed for *zu*, *au* for *ō*, and *ō* for *au*. It would be better, perhaps, always to print *au*. A comma should follow every suspensive and modal, a full stop, colon, or semicolon every conclusive verb or adjective form. *Namu* (*nan*) is sometimes printed separately when it is merely a future auxiliary element. *H* between vowels should be replaced by *y*, except in Chinese words.

Modern Japanese consists, in reality, of two very different languages, pure Japanese and japonicised Chinese or sinico-Japanese.[1] For a full account of the latter, and of the various degrees of the admixture of both that are found in the many styles that characterise Japanese literature, Mr. Aston's admirable treatise, and Mr. Chamberlain's more recent works on the current written language should be consulted. The brief grammatical sketch that follows deals with the pure Japanese of the text alone.[2]

SECTION I.—ORTHOGRAPHY AND PRONUNCIATION.

The orthography adopted in the transliteration of the text is that of the Rōmaji-Kai, a little amplified to reproduce archaic forms. On this system pronunciation becomes a very simple matter; every letter is fully sounded, the consonants as in English, the vowels as in Italian, particular care being given to quantity especially in the case of the long *ō*, which, however, in archaic Japanese was almost always *au* or *ou*. The vowel *u* is equivalent to the Italian *u* in *brutto*, *sullo*, or the English *u* in *put*. The breathing *h* is well sounded, in *hi* it perhaps resembled the Arabic ح. The consonant *g* may be always pronounced hard. The tonic accent, which is not well marked, is penultimate, unless the final syllable is long, when it is final. There is also a euphonic accent like that of Hebrew, with regard to which rules cannot be laid down. All syllables are open, *ts* and *ch* are digraphs.

---

[1] An exacter term would be nipponico- or japonico-Chinese. But both expressions are ill-sounding. The Japanese scholar stands in need of equivalents for such words as sinico, sinicise, and sinologue. Neither nippouologue nor japanologue are satisfactory.

[2] The few Chinese expressions that occur in the text are distinguished in the vocabulary.

Section II.—Grammar of the Noun, Pronoun, and Adjective.

Nouns substantive are destitute of every trace of inflection.

They are simple or compound; *yama* 'hill,' *hara* 'plain,' *fune* 'boat,' *funabito* 'boatman,' *agura* (*age-kura*) 'a sort of raised platform or scaffolding,' *ori-mono* (weave-thing) 'textile fabric.' Some abstract nouns are formed by adding *ge* or *ke* (*ki*='essence, quality'), *nagekashiye* 'causing-grief-ness, painfulness,' etc.; others by suffixing *sa*; perhaps *tsukasa* 'minister, chief, chief servant,' is an instance of this, having originally signified the fact of service merely.

There are but few true pronouns in Japanese. The following list may suffice :—

    1st Person. *a, wa, ware, yo.*
    2nd   „   *na, nare, nanji.*
    3rd   „   *a, are, kare* (that—*is, ille,* Aston).
                 so, sore (that—*iste,* Aston), occasionally *sa.*
                 ko, kore (this—*hic,* Aston).

Interrogative Pronouns.

Ta, tare (*dare*)	'who?'
Na, nani	'what?'
Izu, izure	'which, what?'
Ika (with *naru, ni, nite, ga,* etc.)	'what manner?' ποῖος.
Iku (not in the text)	'what number?' πόσος.

Reflexive Pronouns.

    Shi, onore, mi 'self.' (*Onore* and *mi* are often used for 1st Person.)

    Ono-ono 'every,' *mina* 'all.' There are no Relative Pronouns in Japanese.

Where nouns and pronouns have a plural intent, this is usually left to be inferred from the context, but is indicated by suffixes, forming compounds with a plural sense, where the fact of plurality needs to be emphasised, or where it is desired to mark special groupings. The suffixes used in the text are *ra, tachi,* and *domo.* The etymology of *ra* is unknown; *tachi* is probably the old word for a nobleman's mansion, and has an honorific tinge; *domo* is *tomo* 'company.'

Occasionally the word is repeated to form the plural, thus *hito* 'a man,' *hitobito* 'men,' *i.e.* 'some particular men.' Other suffixes, but less common in Old Japanese, are *kata* (lit. 'side or quarter') and *bara* (etym. uncertain); *nado* (*nani to* contr. of *nani to iu*='what say') means 'and the like, the rest, etcetera.'

Examples : *Sekai no onoko, ate naru mo iyashiki mo* (p. 46) —'Men of the world (*i.e.* of the time), both men of rank and mean men.' *Ki-domo tateri* (p. 49) —'trees were growing there;' *iro-iro no tama* (p. 49) '(different) kinds (kind-kind) of jewels;' *takumi-ra wo iritamaitsutsu* (p. 49)—'his lordship shut up craftsmen and . . . ;' *atari hanarenu kimi-tachi* (p. 46) —'the gentlemen not quitting the neighbourhood;' *uta wo utai . . . ōgi wo narashi nado suru ni*—'in making the singing of songs . . . . the clapping of fans and such like music.'

Numerals: 1 *hito*, 2 *futa*, 3 *mi*, 4 *yo*, 5 *itsu*, 6 *mu*, 7 *nana*, 8 *ya*, 9 *kokono*, 10 *tō* (*tsu?*), 11 *tō amari hito*, 20 *hatachi*, 30 *misoji*, 100 *momochi*, 500 *ihochi*, 1000 *chiji*, 10,000 *yorozu*. To the numerals from 1 to 9 *tsu* is generally added, *hitotsu*, *futatsu*. This *tsu*, according to Mr. Aston, is an old generic suffix, in the remaining forms (save *tō*) represented by *chi*, *ji*. *Hata(chi)*=*fu-to* ('twice ten'), *miso*=*mi to* (or *tsu*), *momo* is simply *tō tō* or 'more-more,' *iho* is *i(tsu)to*. Of *chi* and *yoro* the etymology is unknown. Of the so-called 'auxiliary numerals' only one is found in the text, *take hito suji arikeri* 'there was one stem (*suji*) of bamboo.'

Adjectives are capable of a sort of pseudo-inflexion.[1] There are three forms, consisting of the stem, with the syllables *ku*, *ki*, and *shi* suffixed to it respectively. Thus we have *aka-ku, aka-ki, aka-shi* 'red.' The form in *ku* is adverbial, answering to the suspensive form of verbs,[2] those in *ki* and *shi* answer respectively to the attributive and conclusive forms of the verb. With *ari* agglutinated the adjectives are verbalised and capable of a complete quasi-conjugation.

---

[1] The term inflection should, I think, be limited to processes of internal change (mainly vocalic) of a significant character, not to processes of an agglutinative nature distinct or disguised, so long as the elements are clearly recognizable.

[2] See post.

Examples: *ojinaku, kokoro osonaku, tatsu wo korosamu to* . . . —'foolishly, silly of purpose, designing to kill the dragon.' Chains of adjectives, however, do not often occur in the text; another instance is *yama no sama takaku uruwashi*— 'the appearance of the mountain was loftily beautiful,' *i.e.* lofty and beautiful. *Uruwashi* is contraction, for euphony, of *uruwashishi*. The form in *shi* is not common in the text. An example of *ki* and *shi* is *yama wo miru ni* . . . *noborubeki sama nashi*—'on looking at the mountain—(we saw that) climbable appearance there-was-not' (*nashi*).

A few adjectival locutions in the text are composed of a noun or root combined with the verb *naru*, 'be'; *ate naru* (*hito*) 'rank-be men,' *i.e.* men of breeding and position.

Adverbs and conjunctions can hardly be said to exist, morphologically, in Japanese. The expressions in the text which discharge their functions will be found in the vocabulary, and the mode of formation of some of these will be considered in the section dealing with the particles.

Section III.—Grammar of the Verb.

The Japanese verb shows no true inflection. The so-called conjugations are nothing more than systems of locutions, more or less agglutinated, having modal and temporal functions. It possesses, however, a peculiar but limited morphology, which is neither modal nor temporal in value, but so connects the several verbs of a sentence, when several are present, as to suspend the real significance of the sentence until the last of the chain of verbs is reached. This last verb, which is always the principal verb of the clause or sentence, invariably stands at the end of the clause or sentence. In the former case it is, when not in a modal, in what is termed the indefinite form; in the latter in what is known as the conclusive form. 'Suspensive' is a better designation than 'indefinite,' for the form shows only that the meaning of the sentence is suspended until the final verb is reached. There is a third or 'attributive' form—more strictly, participial—when the verb precedes and qualifies a noun.

Morphologically the suspensive is a stem-form, always

ending in *i* or *e*. The roots of all verbs originally, no doubt, ended in *a*, and this is still the prominent vowel in most verbs, and these the most ancient—in them the stem-form ends in *i*.

Verbs may therefore be classified into: *a* verbs having their stem-form in *i* but changing *i* into *a* in the negative and future forms (Mr. Chamberlain's 1st conjugation); *e* verbs which preserve *e* throughout (Mr. C.'s 2nd conj.); and *i* verbs preserving *i* throughout (Mr. C.'s 3rd and 4th conj.). The *a* verbs further differ from the *e* and *i* verbs in that the primary conclusive and attributive forms are identical; in the *e* and *i* verbs the attributive end in *uru* and *iru* respectively, and the conclusive in *u*, but in four monosyllabic [1] *i* verbs (given below, and constituting Mr. C.'s 4th conj.) the conclusive and attributive forms both terminate in *iru*.

Of these three classes the following paradigm shows the quasi-inflectional primary forms respectively: [2]—

	Suspensive.	Conclusive.	Attributive.
a verbs (*yaka* 'burn')	*yaki* (burn)	*yaku* (burn)	*yaku* (burn)
e verbs (*home* 'praise')	*home* (praise)	*homu*	*homuru*
i verbs (*sugi* 'pass')	*sugi* (pass)	*sugu*	*suguru*.
Mr. Chamberlain's 4th conjug.			
i	*i*	*iru*	*iru*
ni	*ni*	*niru*	*niru*
mi	*mi*	*miru*	*miru*
hi	*hi*	*hiru*	*hiru*
ki	*ki*	*kiru*	*kiru* [3]

[1] The most ancient words in Japanese and nearly all the verbs are dissyllabic, indeed biliteral. There is good reason to regard Japanese as not being a monosyllabic language, though, originally, it seems to have been nearly as analytic as Chinese.

[2] Of this and the following paradigms the materials are taken from Mr. Chamberlain's Grammar.

[3] There are three verbs *i*, having each a different meaning; two verbs *ni*; three verbs *hi*; one verb *mi*; and one verb *ki*. See Mr. Chamberlain's Grammar, p. 66.

To the above may be added the emphatic (past) form, in *e*, *yake*, *homure*, *sugure*, *mire* used with the particle *koso*; *yake* is also used as an imperative.

In the next paradigm will be found the agglutinated, non-auxiliary, quasi-conjugational forms—

	a verb (*yaka* 'burn').	*e* verb (*home* 'praise').	*i* verbs (*sugi* 'pass,' *mi* 'see').
Future.	*yakamu*[1] (*yakan*) 'shall burn'	*homemu* (*homen*)	*sugimu* *mimu.* (*sugin*) (*min*)
Past Participle.	*yakite*[2] 'having burnt'	*homete*	*sugite* *mite.*
Conditional.	*yakeba*[3] 'as, since, when, burn'	*homureba*	*sugureba* *mireba.*
Hypothetical.	*yakaba*[4] 'if, should, burn'	*homeba*	*sugiba* *miba.*

There is also a negative form which will be considered separately later on. These modal forms are never suspensive, conclusive, or attributive.

Lastly, of the three principal irregular verbs *ara* 'be,' *ko* 'come,' *shi* (*se*) 'do,' the paradigms are—

Suspensive	*ari* (be)	*ki*	*shi.*
Conclusive.	*ari* [not *aru*] (be)	*kuru* (*ku?*)	*su.*
Attributive.	*aru* (be)	*kuru*	*suru.*
Emphatic.	*are* (be)		
Future.	*aramu* (shall be ?)	*komu* (*kon*)	*semu* (*sen*).
Past Participle.	*arite* (having been)	*kite*	*shite.*
Conditional.	*areba* (since, as &c., be)		
Hypothetical.	*araba* (if, should, be)	*koba*	*seba.*

The auxiliary forms result from the agglutination of the different forms of certain verbs and adjectives. The verbs —chiefly *ari* 'be,' *ki* 'come,' *shi* (*suru*, *su*) 'do,' *ni* 'be,' *ini* 'go away,' and *ye we* (*uru*) 'get'—are agglutinated to the suspensive form of the principal verb; the adjectives—chiefly *beku* 'able,' and *taku* 'wishful,' are added—the former to the conclusive, the latter to the suspensive form of the principal

---

[1] *mu* = perhaps *mi* 'see.' Comp. forms in *me*, *meri*, explained in Notes.
[2] This may be auxiliary—*te* = a form of *tsu* preserved perhaps in *tōri* 'pass on.'
[3] *yakeba* = *yake wa*. See Particles, *wa*.
[4] *yakaba* — *yaka wa*.

verb. These various auxiliaries may be piled one on the top of the other. In all cases the vowel changes are quite simple, and though the agglutinations are often cumbrous enough, the elements are always easily recognisable. In fact the analysis of the verbal forms and locutions throughout presents no difficulty to the student who is familiar with their elements.

The most important of these auxiliary agglutinations are those which give a preterite sense. They are shown in the following paradigm—C signifying the conclusive, A the attributive form.

a verbs.

C *yakeri* (yaki-ari)
A *yakeru* (yaki-aru)
C *yakiki* (yaki-ki)
A *yakishi* (yaki-shi)
C *yakitari* (yakite-ari)   'burnt,'
A *yakitaru* (yakite-aru)   'did burn,'
C *yakitariki* (yakite-ari-ki)   'have burnt,'
A *yakitarishi* (yakite-ari-shi)   'had burnt,' etc.
C *yakinu* (yaki-ni or ini)
A *yakinuru* (yaki-nuru or inuru)
C *yakikeri* (yaki-ki-ari)
A *yakikeru* (yaki-ki-aru)

Replacing *yaki* and *yake* by *home*, we have a paradigm of *e* verbs; by *sugi* or *mi*, of *i* verbs.

With some of these forms the modal agglutinations (*e*)*ba*, (*a*)*ba*, etc., can be compounded. Those that occur in the text will be explained, when needful, in the analysis and notes that follow, or in the vocabulary. This agglutination is especially common when the final auxiliary is *ari*. Thus we have *yakitareba, yakitaraba, yakitaredomo*,[1] and a whole quasi-conjugation of *bekari* (*beku-ari*) and *takari* (*taku-ari*). The

forms $\frac{yakubeku}{yakitaku}$ (suspensive), $\frac{yakubeshi}{yakitashi}$ (conclusive)

$\frac{yakubeki}{yakitaki}$ (attributive) are really compound adjectives.

[1] The explanation of this form will be found in the section on the particles.

The negative form of the Japanese verb is constructed by suffixing *nu* [1] to the root in *a, e,* or *i*. Thus; *yakanu, homenu,*[2] *suginu,*[2] *minu.*[2] The modal forms change *nu* into *neba, nedomo*; *naba* is not found, but *nete* (past participle), originally perhaps *nite,* becomes *de.* Thus : *yakaneba, yakanedomo, yakade.*[3] So with *home, sugi, mi.* To *nu, su (shi, ·suru)* is added to form another negative base, *n'su* contracted into *zu,* and to this *ari* may be subjoined. Thus we have such forms as *yakazu*[4] (conclusive), *yakazaru* (attributive), *yaka-zarishi, yakazaramu(n), yakazareba,* etc. There is also a future form in *ji, yakaji,* and the hypothetical instead of ending in *-naba* or *-zaraba* is constructed with the conclusive in *zu* and the particle *wa*—thus *yakazu-wa* euphonised into *yaka-zu(m)ba.*

In the text the archaic model *na yaki so* is usually followed for the negative imperative.

Instead of *bekarazu* the adjective *majiku* may be suffixed to the conclusive form—

yaku [5] {	*majiku*	indefinite
	maji (mai)	conclusive
	majiki	attributive
	majikariki	part conclusive
	majikarishi	part attributive
	majikereba	conditional
	majikuba	hypothetical
	majikeredomo	concessive

Ari (be)+*uru* (attributive of *ye, e,* get) agglutinated with a verb-stem construct a quasi-passive conjugated as an *e* verb. Thus : *yakaruru (yaka-ari-uru), homeraruru (home-ari-uru), sugiraruru, miraruru.* The interpolated *r* of the last three forms is either euphonic or the remnant of an additional *ari.*

<hr>

[1] The etymology of *nu* is unknown. Perhaps it is simply *(i)nu(ru)* to go away in the sense of ceasing. In Japanese the idea of not-being is less involved in the negative than the notion of ceasing to be.
[2] Identical *in form* with the past in *nu.*
[3] Or perhaps *yakanu-te* or *yakazu-te.*
[4] This form is also used as equivalent to the past participle: *yakazu=yakade.*
[5] See Mr. Chamberlain's Grammar. Not all of these forms are found in the text.

Or *uru* alone may be added—thus *miyuru* 'get-see, seem,' where the *y* is an inorganic addition—giving a sense varying from intransitive to passive. Forms of *shi* (*su*, *suru* 'do') are agglutinated to construct causative verbs, such as *shimuru*, *seshimuru*, *sasuru*. Thus *yakashimuru, tsukurasuru* (cause to burn, make), etc.

Very curious compounds result from these various agglutinations, such as the more modern *araseraruru* = *ari* + *shi* (*se-* 'do')+*ari*+*ari*+(*ye-e, uru*, 'get'), lit. 'get the being of the being caused to be,' used as an honorific for *ari*.[1] The following is a perfectly legitimate word ; *hayakarashimubeka-razaredomo* 'although should (could) not cause to be early (or swift).' Other forms are *arawaru, arawaseru*, etc. These quasi-passives have sometimes a potential force, but this is more commonly the case in the later than in the archaic language.

The verb *ni* 'be' requires a word or two. Its forms are the past participle *nite*, the future *namu* (*nan*), and the agglutinated *ni* + *ari* = *nari*, *naru*. *Ni* is often an element of a past form—*nige-ni-keri nige* + *ni* + *ki* + *ari*, 'he, etc., ran away.' *Nari* (*u*) has evolved two meanings, 'be'[2] and 'become.' When it has the latter, it is preceded by the particles *ni* or *to*. *Nari* (conclusive) 'be, is' often merely closes a sentence, an articulate full stop as it were. *Naru* affixed to word-stems forms compound adjectival expressions, *akiraka-naru* 'bright.' For the negative of *ni* the adjective *naku, naki, nashi* is used with agglutination of *ari* to the first form *nakari, nakareba, nakaramu*(*n*), etc.

Section IV.—Grammar of the Particles.

The particles in Japanese are of great importance, and perfect the expression of thought in a manner and to a degree unknown in Chinese, and somewhat reminding one of the completeness of Greek.

They are words used occasionally or wholly as particles, or remnants of words used as particles only.

---

[1] Mr. Chamberlain's Grammar, p. 83.
[2] Or 'be in' or 'be of.'

Functionally they are *syndesma* (σύνδεσμος) linking together words, propositions, clauses, and sentences.

Only the principal particles will be here considered. Of these the most important are the monosyllables *wa*, *wo*, *no* (*ga*, *tsu*), *ni*, *to*, *mo*, and *zo*. *Wa* emphasises the word or phrase it follows as a prominent element of the thought expressed. *Miko wa kokoro tabakari aru hito nite, ōyake ni wa Tsukushi . . . . ni makaramu tote, itōma moshite, Kaguya Hime no iye ni wa tama no yeda tori ni namu makaru to iwasete. . . .* "The PRINCE (*miko wa*), crafty fellow as he was, PUBLICLY (*ōyake ni wa*) gave out he was off to Tsukushi, and took leave, BUT AT THE HOUSE OF THE LADY KAGUYA (*iye ni wa*) caused it to be reported that he had gone to fetch the jewel-branch." *Wo* has a similar meaning to that of *wa*, but shows what the thought (action or passion) moves to, *wa* rather what it moves from. Much the most frequently it is a syndesmos between a transitive verb and the object— *yama wo miru ni* 'on looking at the mountain;' *Dainagon kore wo kikite* 'the D. having heard this.' But the verb may be intransitive or even quasi-passive. Where the connection is very close as in such an expression as *itōma mōshite*, which might be written *itōma-mōshite* 'having taken leave' (lit. having spoken, *i.e.* requested, leisure), *wo* is often omitted. The object is not necessarily a noun; *tsuki no omoshirō idetaru wo mite* (p. 56), 'having seen the moon's delightful rising.' *Wo* may be omitted too when the verbal action is more or less continuous; as in *nawo kono onna mide wa* (p. 48), 'now as he continued not to see this woman' (Kaguya). *Wo* also serves but rarely as an adversative syndesmos between clauses—here, however, there is probably some ellipsis—and, especially in poetry, it is occasionally an interjection.

With *wa—wo ba*—a sort of double emphasis results; *na wo ba Sanugi . . . to namu iikeru* (p. 46), 'as to his name (*na wa*) that ((*na*) *wo*) they called Sanugi.'

No is the common generic syndesmos connecting most frequently two nouns so as to turn the first into an attributive of the second; *yama no michi* 'the mountain-road' (generally), or (particularly) 'the road to or by, etc., the mountain ;' *tama no yeda* 'jewel's branch,' *i.e.* jewel-branch ; *hime no iu yō*, . . . 'the Lady's speak-way,' *i.e.* what the Lady said was . . . ; *ichi no takumi*, ' (number) one's craftsman,' *i.e.* the first of craftsmen ; *tatsu no kubi no tama*, 'dragon's head's jewel,' *i.e.* the jewel in the dragon's head. The adjectival use of *no* is very common. Sometimes a chain of substantives is linked by *no* to a sequent one; *umi yama no michi* (p. 48)=*umi no michi yama no michi*.

No may connect other words than nouns. It may indeed be linked with the preceding or following phrase—*yo-nó-naka-ni-naki-hana no ki* 'world's-within-not-exist-flowers'-trees'=trees bearing flowers the like of which the world has not; *kono hitobito no toshi-tsuki-hete-kō-nomi-imashitsutsu* (p. 47), 'these men's year-month-traversed-thus-not-elsewise-have remained,' where the *no* is a syndesmos between *hito-hito* and the verb *imashitsutsu* qualified by the intervening words.

Ga is rare in the text—*ono ga nasanu ko nareba*, 'as (she) is not my own child . . . ;' *ono ga mi wa* (p. 55), 'as to mine own self. . . .' In *Maro ga mōsu yo* (p. 54) *ga* appears to be a miscopying for *no*; it does not seem to be an instance of the more modern use of *ga* (Aston, p. 118).

Tsu is found in such expressions as *mitsu (zu) kara, ono-zu kara*, etc. = *mi no karada, ono karada*, 'oneself's body,' *i.e.* oneself.

Ni has dative, locative (dynamic or static), instrumental, gerundial, participial, and adverbial functions— *Ware ni musme wo tabe*, ' to us (or one of us) give the girl ;' *kaki ni mo to ni mo oru hito*, 'the men who remained at (about) the fence and at (about) the door ;' *iye ni kayerite*, ' having returned to the house ;' *kore wo mite oru ni*, ' after having regarded it for awhile ;' *ōgi wo narashi nado suru ni*, ' in doing fan-clappings and such-like . . . ;' *itazura ni, sara ni, naka ni, ōki ni*, 'vainly, certainly, inly (within), greatly.' In the subjoined sentence various uses of *ni* are exemplified—*Hime suyemu ni wa, rei no yō ni wa, minikushi to notamaite*, ... *ya no uye ni wa, ito wo somete, iroiro ni fukasete, uchiuchi no shitsurai ni wa iubeku mo arazu aya orimomo ni ye wo kakite ma goto ni haritari*

(p. 52), 'as for the Lady's lodging, as for the ordinary furnishing thereof, it was altogether ill to see said (the Dainagon) . . . . . . now on the top of the roof, (men) having dyed silk, they roofed over the roof with all sorts of coloured silks; next, as to the preparation of the interior of the mansion, it is impossible to describe it, on damasks and silks (men) limned pictures, and with such they hung the rooms severally' (*goto ni*), *i.e.* all the rooms without exception.

To is perhaps an old form of *tsu* (compare *toki*, old form of *tsuki* 'moon'). It is best rendered by the conjunctive 'that'—*nochi kuyashiki koto arubeki wo* [1] *to omou bakari nari* (p. 49), 'I just think that afterwards there would be regretfulness.' It especially precedes verbs of thinking, speaking, seeing, etc.; with *shi (suru, su)* 'to do,' it indicates tendency, purpose, etc.—*magiremu to shi . . . kui-kakaramu to shiki* (p. 49), 'made for disappearing (seemed about to disappear) . . . made for falling upon and devouring us' (were on the point of falling, etc.). In all these cases *to* has a quotative or quasi-quotative function in reference to what precedes. Sometimes it gives an adverbial function to the preceding word—*mera-mera to yake ni shikaba*, 'since crackle-crackleingly it was burnt up and consumed.' Very often the value of *to* is best reached by rendering it first as 'thus'— *kore to chigau*,[2] 'this, thus, differ,' *i.e.* it is different from this. *To* may also be a copulative conjunction, but this function is not exemplified in the text.

Mo, 'even, also, too,' often a mere emphatic—*okashiki koto ni mo aru kana!* (p. 53), 'O what a pleasant thing, too, it is, to be sure!' *Morokoshi ni mo nakarikeru* (p. 51), 'not even in Morokoshi (China) was it to be found;' *nagori naku mo* (p. 51), 'without the least vestige (remaining);' *mono mo iwazu*, 'saying nothing at all,' *i.e.* not a word. *To mo* gives often a hypothetical concessive meaning to the preceding verb, *nari tomo* 'if it were,' but not always; *sa wa mosu to mo haya yakite*, etc. (p. 51), seems to mean simply, 'so 'tis said, then let them burn, etc.' *Mo* is common after *ni* and

---

[1] *Wo* here has an interjectional function.
[2] Mr. Aston's Grammar.

wo; it is not often conjoined with *wa*, *ga*, *no*. With *to* it combines to form *domo*, the ordinary (non-hypothetical) concessive form. Frequently, especially in the later language, suffixed to *kere* (*ki*+*ari*)—*keredomo*.

Zo is purely an emphatic particle, somewhat like the Greek γε—*kore wo kiite zo togenaki mono wo ba* 'abenashi' *to iyeru*, 'having heard this, at once (*zo*) as to luckless thing it (men) dubbed *abenashi*;' *yorozu no asobi wo zo shikeru* (p. 46), 'ten thousand diversions, in fact, they practised.'

Koso is more emphatic still, resembling the Greek ἤτοι. The uses of this particle are indicated in the analysis and notes subjoined. It often gives the force almost of the Greek perfect imperative.

Ka, *ya* are interrogative particles, placed generally at the end of the sentence. Following words, especially pronouns, in the body of a sentence, they give an indefinite sense to them. *Ka wa*, *ya wa* are equivalent to the Latin *num*, implying a negative answer. *Koyasu no gai toritaru ka*, 'have they taken the cowry shell?' *to kiku wa makoto ka* (p. 54), 'what one hears is it true?' *Okina no mōsamu hito kiki-tamaiten ya*, 'will you not (have) listen(ed) just to what the old man says,' *i.e.* he prays you hearken to his word; *nani ni ka wa semu* (p. 58), 'shall I make anything whatever of it?' *i.e.* what will it boot me! *kare ya . . . waga yama naramu to omoite*, 'thinking that perhaps might be my mountain;' *nani no yō ni ka aramu*, 'for what sort of purpose will it be?' *tsui ni otoko awasezaramu ya wa to omoite* (p. 47), 'thinking would she for ever disdain a husband (no, she would not);' *ikayō naru kokorozashi aramu hito ni ka awamu to obosu* (p. 47), 'with whatever-sort-of-a-disposition-having-man then think you to mate.' In the last example the *ka* is almost superfluous, it gives the tinge of a sneer. *Ka*, *ya* also serve as disjunctives, but not in the text.

Kana, or *gana*, is an interjection of surprise, admiration, or grief, at the end of the sentence, often preceded by *mo*, commoner in archaic poetry than in archaic prose. The remaining particles will be found sufficiently explained in the following pages.

Section V.—Syntax.

But a brief sketch of the syntax of archaic Japanese can be here given. The main features are the relegation of a commonly subjectless [1] verb to the end of the clause or sentence, the replacement of relative clauses by adjectival polysynthetisms, and the tendency of the sentence to assume a complex structure by the piling-up of clauses, adjectival, or connected by quasi-modal verb-forms, or by particles, in a sequence of successive modification, which easily becomes cumbrous and obscure. The following slightly complex sentence fairly illustrates the general structure of the language.

Ware 'I,' *asa* 'morning,' *goto* 'severally,' *yū* 'evening,' *goto ni* 'severally,' *miru* 'see,' *take no* 'bamboos',' *naka ni* 'within' (or among), *owasuru* 'exist,' *nite* 'having been,' *shirinu* 'have known,' *ko* 'child,' *ni naritamobeki* 'becomable,' *hito* 'person,' *nameri* 'seems,' *i.e.* this person would seem properly to be considered as a child (whom) I have known (*i.e.* my child), having been (being) existent among these bamboos (which) I behold every evening and every morning.

Here *nameri* is the principal verb, *hito* qualified by all that precedes is the predicate and no subject is expressed; *kono mono wa* may be taken to be understood as beginning the sentence. When expressed the subject is usually indicated by the postposition *wa* and the object by the postposition *wo*. At the end of a sentence the verb is invariably in the conclusive form, at the end of a clause it may be in the suspensive, or in a quasi-modal form. A chain of suspensive forms, together with the conclusive verb, may be regarded as a compound verb denoting a group of associated actions or states—*kakareba kono hitobito iye ni kayerite, mono wo omoi-, inori wo shi-, guwan wo tate-, omoi-yamemu to suredomo yamubeku mo arazu,* " things being thus, although these (particular) men after having returned (*kayerite*) to their

---

[1] Of course there is always a logical subject at least to be extracted from the context.

mansions made for stopping (sought to stop) their griev(ing), their supplicat(ing), their petition(ing), their keep(ing)-their-thoughts-upon (the Lady) there was no possibility of stopping." It is as if, the order of structure being reversed in English, the termination 'ing' were omitted from 'griev-,' 'supplicat-,' 'petition-,' etc., and supplied from the first 'stopping.' The whole phrase from *mono* to *suredomo* inclusive must be regarded as a polysynthetism. In the text there are instances where the suspensive chain is closed by a participial form (in *te*), by future and by post forms, but none in which it is closed by a negative or modal one.[1] In the attributive form the verb is adjectival to the noun following; or to *koto* or *mono* understood, as, for instance, when the sentence terminates with an interrogative or interjectional particle (*ka, ya, kana, wo*). Where a preceding *clause* is adjectival to a noun,[2] the attributive form does not seem necessary—*yoru wo akashi, hi wo kurasu hito ōkari* (p. 46), 'many were the men who saw the night through to day and the day through to dark;' here *hito* is qualified by *yoru* . . . . . *kurasu* and *kurasu* is conclusive in form. So p. 47, *rei no atsumarinu* (not *atsumarinuru*) *hitobito, yoru wa yasuki i mo nezu,* '(They) by night (did) not find rest in sleep;' *yami no yo ni idete mo,* 'in the dark night, too, sallying forth;' *ana wo kujiri* '(did) bore holes;' *koko kashiko yori nozoki,* 'through here and there (did) peep;' *kaimami madoi ayeri,* '(did) peep, (did) become-distracted, did-so-all-together.' Here *nezu* (neg. suspensive[3]), *kujiri, nozoki, kaimami, madoi* must all be read as though each had the post termination *eri* of *ayeri,*[4] or its equivalent. In fact the whole phrase is polysynthetic.

Inversion for emphasis is occasionally met with, especially in poetry. An example of prose inversion will be found on p. 49—*ikanaru tokoro ni ka, kono ki wa, soraikemu ?=kono*

---

[1] The suspensive form is also used as the Greek infinitive often is with τὸ— *yō nuki ariki wa,* τό ἀχρῆστως περιπατεῖν.

[2] A characteristic construction in Greek and German, and not unknown in English. In Japanese, as in Chinese, it obtains universally, in the former language, as is more fully shown a little further on, to the point of obscurity.

[3] In negative verbs the conclusive and suspensive forms are alike.

[4] Or *kaimami-madoi-ayeri* may be regarded as a compound verb.

ki wa, ikanaru tokoro ni soraikemu ka? 'in what sort of a place will this tree (or these trees) have been (found), Sir?' Qualifying words or phrases precede the words or phrases qualified; postpositions are no exception, for they are, as already stated, links, *syndesma*. It is this relegation of the verb to the end, combined with the lack of relative pronouns, that makes the Japanese compound sentence somewhat difficult at first to seize and unravel the meaning of—the pivot of the sentence being the verb, the real significance of it is kept in abeyance until the chain of constituent clauses and their relations are taken into cognisance. There is, however, something to be said for the Japanese structure as a mode of stating the elements of the thought in ascending order of importance culminating in the verb; it is the absence of relative pronouns that prevents breaks being made and tends to induce complexity by involving clause within clause as in the sentence (p. 48)—*Tōchi no kōri ni aru yamadera ni Binzuru no maye naru hachi no hitakuro ni suzukitaru (hachi) wo torite,* 'having taken (a vase which was) blackened with soot among the vases before Binzuru('s altar) in a hill temple which was in the district of Tochi.'

Read with the foregoing observations the analysis and notes that follow will sufficiently explain the syntax of the text. The difficulties of structure soon disappear, especially if the conclusive forms being first determined these are marked off by a full stop or semicolon, and the modal and suspensive forms by a comma. The subjects, however, of the different verbs in a compound sentence are not always easy to find, being more often implied than expressed; in fact Japanese hardly ever fully expresses the thought, and cannot at all express the fine shades of meaning attached to the temporal and modal forms of the Aryan verb. This is especially the case when several of the subordinate clauses of the sentence are quotative—there is no oblique narration in Japanese—as will be seen in the Ancient's speech to the suitors on p. 47, beginning *katajikenaku mo,* etc., and explained below (p. 83).

Enough has been said on the syntax of the principal
syndesma (*wa, wo, no,* etc.) in the section dealing with these.
Care must always be taken with *no* to determine whether it
links on to the word immediately following, or to some word
further removed and qualified by an intervening clause—in
other words to the following clause; as in the sentence
katachi no yo ni nizu medetaki koto, ' Her (Kaguya's) form's
not-in-the-world-like loveliness,' *i.e.* ' her incomparable loveliness.'

The participial form in *te* is often best rendered by the
English past followed by 'and'—*irite iwaku,* 'he went in and
said.'

The future followed by *to suru*[1] (or *tote*) indicates purpose
or endeavour—*yamemu to suredomo,* 'although they did (made
for)—*i.e.* wished or tried to—end (their grief).' A few
examples of the use of the common modal forms (*eba, aba,
domo, tomo*) are subjoined. *Te wo suri notamayeba* "*ono ga
nasanu ko nareba*—(p. 47)," 'as they rubbed their hands
(suppliant-wise) and said . . . . . (the old man answered)
since she is a child not-begot by myself.' *Ada-kokoro
tsukinaba* (p. 47), ' in the event of mating with a fickle-
hearted one.' *Ihe ni yukitetatazumi-ariki keredomo . . . .
fumi wo kakite yaredomo . . . ,* 'though they went to the
house and stopped and paced up and down . . . . and wrote
epistles and despatched them (as they actually did) . . . . ;'
mo or *tomo* with the attributive form would mean 'should
they (by any chance) go to the house and there dally and
walk about, etc.' In Japanese the mere position of a clause
relative to others never gives it a conditional or concessive
force as in Chinese.

The negative element is always included in the verb and
cannot be isolated or attached to a noun. There is thus no
word for ' not ' in Japanese.

In strictness there is no past form of the Japanese verb,
unless what is called above the 'emphatic' form be so regarded.
In that case with *koso* it would resemble the Greek perfect

---

[1] Compare the Greek ποιεῖν ὥστε with infinitive.

imperative. The conclusive *yaku, homu,* etc., are logically
past or future or present in accordance with the context.
Whenever, however, it is desired to express the past time
with some particularity or emphasis, or to avoid obscurity,
one of the past forms, all constructed with suffixed auxiliaries,
is used. Of these the syntax has not been much studied.
In the text the form in *keri, keru,* seems to imply more than
a momentary state or act; that in *tari taru* to be aoristic
having relation mainly to events; that in *nu nuru* to denote
a concluded action, etc. The forms in *eri eru* (compare
amavi = ama + fui), and in *ki, shi,* cannot clearly be distinguished from each other in relation to their functions.

Other past forms occurring in the text will be found
explained in the notes.

Modern Japanese, Mr. Chamberlain tells us, is saturated
with the honorific spirit—with the self-depreciatory spirit
as well it might be added. In the archaic language also,
but in more moderate measure, honorifics and humilifics are
found. The honorifics of nouns—there are no humilifics—
are *mi* and *on* or *ohon.*[1] Both perhaps are worn down
remainders of *ohomi,* grand. *Mi* indicates what pertains to
the Mikado, *on* is employed in other cases. To verbs
honorifics are never prefixed as in the modern language.
The suffixed honorifics and humilifics are all of the nature of
auxiliary verbs. The principal auxiliary honorifics are:

tama(w)i—root *tamawa,* meaning originally 'to bestow,'
as in the sentence already quoted (p. 70), *ware ni musume
wo tabe (tame).* It is used generally with verbs, denoting
some action or state of, or connected with, the individual
honoured — *tamahe, tamau, tamawaru, tamaheba, tamaite,
tamaine, tamawazu, tamawarazu, tamawarazaramu, tamaiki,*
are the commonest forms in the text.

mashi (masu, maseri, masenu, etc.) is said to be a verbalised
Chinese vocable. In the text it is met with solely in the
verb *owashimasu,* 'to cause to be,' a derivative of *i* 'be in or

---

[1] The Chinese *go* is met with in a few instances, chiefly as an honorific to
Chinese verbs.

at a place,' etc. (Spanish 'estar'), and signifying 'Your, or
IIis Majesty, Grace, Lordship, etc., is' or 'is in or at.'—
or asserting existence of something pertaining or having
reference to the person honoured.

The principal humilific auxiliaries are:

tatematsuri (*a* verb) 'to present, offer up to.'

tsukamatsuri (*a* verb) 'to render service to.'

haberi (*a* verb) 'to be beside, be in attendance upon,' sometimes used separately as a mere copula. It is the archaic
equivalent of the modern *sōrō*. *Mōsu, mōshi*, (*a* verb) 'to
address,' also used separately in that sense, when an auxiliary
is attached to verbs of 'declaring,' 'denying,' and the
like. *Sōrō, sōrai*[1] (*a* verb) had the same meaning as *haberi*,
in the modern epistolary style it seems to be *de rigueur*
to attach it wherever possible. In the text it is used in
its original sense once—*tsukasa sōrō hitobito mina* (p. 50),
'the officers and retainers of his household all . . . . ;' and
once as a verb signifying existence or position—*ikanaru
tokoro ni ka kono ki wa sōraikemu* 'in what sort of a place,
I wonder, will this tree have been growing.'

The causative and quasi-passive forms, to avoid direct
assertion (which Greek also dislikes), are often used in an
honorific sense.

Two compounds of *tamau* are very common; *notamau*, 'to
say,' used with reference to the person honoured, and *uketamawaru*, 'to receive or hear,' used with reference to the
speaker or some one regarded as inferior to some third
person. *uketamawaru* is a quasi-passive form, and would
be literally rendered 'to get bestowed upon one,' hence the
tamau is really honorific, not humilific.

Occasionally honorific and humble auxiliaries are combined
—*aitatematsuri-tamaine* 'be pleased to courteously grant an
interview.' IIere *tamaine* indicates a favour to be accorded
(by Kaguya) to the speaker (the Bamboo-IIewer), and *tatematsuri* the courtesy due (from Kaguya) to the suitors.

---

[1] Originally *samurai* or *saburai*.

ANALYSIS OF THE TEXT OF 'KAGUYA HIME NO OITACHI.'

Kaguya Hime no oi-tachi, the Lady Kaguya's growing-up.

Ima wa mukashi, now formerly (once upon a time)—*muka-shi* is connected with *mukai*, 'turn towards,' here turning towards the past, looking back. The phrase is a common commencement of stories of all kinds; a more familiar one is *mukashi mukashi*.

Taketori no Okina to iyeru mono arikeri, 'there existed one of those fellows whom (men) call Old Bamboo-Hewer(s).' *Iyeru* is a past attrib. form of *ii* 'to say,' 'call.' *arikeri* is *ari-ki-ari*, a conclus. auxil. past of *aru*. *To* is 'that,' contained in 'whom.'

Shigeyama ni majirite take wo toritsutsu, In the bushy hills he busied himself and took bamboos and thereupon . . . , *majirite* p. part. *majiri*=lit. get or be in among. *tsutsu* connects action of verb with action next following.

Yorozu no koto ni tsukaikeri, to serve ten thousand purposes (litt. *res*) fashioned them, 'to serve . . . . fashioned' is the meaning of *tsukai*.

Na wo ba Sanugi no Miyakko to namu iikeru, as to (his) name men called (it) indeed (*namu*) Sanugi no Miyakko. Note the construction *wo ba* for *wo wa*, the accus. *na wo* isolated for emphasis' sake by *wa*.

Sono take no naka ni, among those bamboos, *i.e.* those amid which the Ancient laboured.

moto hikaru take hito suji arikeri, a self-shining bamboo one stem there was. *ayashigarite yorite miru ni*, (he was) astonished and approached, and on looking (videndo) at (the shining reed), *tsutsu no naka hikaritari* (he saw that), the interior of the hollow-stem was filled with light, *sore wo mireba*, and as he gazed on this (light), *san sun bakari naru hito ito utsukushiute itari*, (he saw that) a human being (*hito*) of about three inches of exceeding beauty stood in it. Note the use of *te* with the suspensive form of the adjective *utsu-kushi(k)u* giving it a verbal force, so that the phrase might be translated 'displaying great beauty . . .'

Okina iu yō, The Ancient-speak-wise, *i.e.* the Ancient thus spoke.

Ware asa goto yū goto ni miru take no naka ni owasuru nite, as (it) deigns-to-be within this bamboo which I see each morning and each evening. *Nite* is here probably the p. part. of *naru*, be.

Shirinu ko ni naritamōbeki hito nameri, it looks as though the being might become (might be taken to be) my own child. *Shirinu*,[1] translated 'my own,' is the conclusive past of *shiri*, know. *Ko* perhaps involves a word-play, meaning both a child and a basket such as it was the Ancient's craft to fashion. *Nameri=name-ari, name* being emphatic future (or dubitative) form in *e* of *naru*, be.

Tote, te ni uchi-irete motte kinu, so saying he put her in his hand and took her and came (to his house). For *kinu* one would have expected *kite*, taking it as part of the next sentence.

Me no ōna ni azukarite yashinawasu, and gave her in charge of his wife's women, and caused her to be brought up.

Utsukushiki koto kagiri-nashi, ito osanakereba ko ni irete yashinau, the beautiful-ness was without end, as (she) was extremely young (they) placed her in a basket and cherished her.

Taketori no Okina take toru ni kono ko wo mitsukete nochi ni take toru ni fushi wo hedatete, the Old Hewer after having set eyes upon this child in the course of his bamboo-taking, in (still) taking bamboos split up the joints and . . .

yo goto ni kogane aru take wo mitsukuru koto kasanarinu, night after night there accumulated his setting-eyes-upon (he continued to set eyes on) a bamboo full of gold.

Kakute Okina yōyō yutaka ni nari-yuku, Thus (it was and) the Ancient finally arrived at opulence. *Yōyō (yaya, yōyaku)* may be taken here as 'finally.'

Kono chigo yashinau hodo ni sugusugu to ōkini nari-masaru. In measure as (*hodo ni*) they brought up this child, rapidly it grew up to be big.

---

[1] It does not seem necessary that this should be read *shirinuru*, the whole phrase being the attribute of *ko*.

Mi-tsuki bakari ni naru hodo ni yoki hodo naru hito ni narinureba kami-age nado sadashite kami-age-sesase mo gisu, chō no uchi yori idasazu. As (the girl—the use of the word *utsukushi* has shown that the child was a girl) became about three months old and already attained (the appearance of a) person of full age (*yoki hodo*, i.e. good or marriageable age) the lifting of tresses, etc., was thereupon arranged and the lifting of tresses accomplished and the maiden's gown (*mo*) put on, but she was not put forth from within the curtain. This is a most instructive sentence. Note: *naru*, be,—*yoki hodo naru hito*; *naru*, become— .... *hito ni narinureba*, the five verbal forms—*naru* attrib., *naru*, again attrib., *narinureba* temporal and modal, *sadashite* p. part., *sesase* honorific double causative, suspensive,—leading up to the conclusive form *gisu* (*kisu*); *narinureba* is a conditional form of the past *narinuru = nari-inuru*, where *inuru* (go away) gives the meaning of *just as she became.* The active verbs have been rendered by passive verbs in English, as is often necessary in translating Japanese, especially where, as in the present case, there is some confusion of implied subjects.

Itsuki-kashizuki-yashinau hodo ni. (They) brought (her) up with lovingness (*itsuki*) and carefulness (*kashizuki*) and so (*hodo ni*), *kono chigo no katachi kyōra naru koto yo ni naku ya no uchi wa kuraki tokoro naku hikari-michitari*, the form of this child was of a loveliness (*kyōra*) this world cannot show (lit. lacking in this world), within the house was no gloomy place (but) it was filled with light. Note the suspensive adjectival forms in *ku* leading up to the conclusive past verbal form in *tari*. *Itsuki-kashizuki-yashinau* is a tricomposite verb, the first two elements are in the suspensive form.

Okina kokochi ashiku kurushiki toki mo kono ko wo mireba. Even (*mo*) when (*toki*) the old man's feelings (*kokochi*) were painful and sad, as he gazed upon the child *kurushiki koto mo yaminu* even the sadness ceased, *haradatashiki koto mo nagusamikeri*, and annoyance was replaced by agreeableness. The full sentence would be *Okina wa kokochi, etc., toki ni*, but to give a certain emphatic rapidity these (and other) particles are omitted in the text. The conclusive form *yaminu*

gives a strength to the phrase that would have been
absent had the suspensive *yami* been employed. *Okina take
wo toru koto hisashiku nari*; the ancient's bamboo-taking went
on for a long time, *ikioi mō no mono ni nari ni keri*, he became
a flourishing and influential personage.

Kono ko ōki narinureba, as this child finished becoming
of full stature, *na wo ba Mimuro Imube no Akita wo yobite
tsukesasu*, (they) made give a name and called her Mimuro,
etc., *Akita naoyotake no Kaguya Hime to tsuketsu*, and gave
her the title of Akita, etc.—*tsu* = the past *nu*. *Kono hodo mi
ka uchi-age-asobu, yorozu no asobi wo zo shikeru*. At this
juncture for three days (they) lifted up the bowl and revelled
and enjoyed, in fact, ten thousand revelries.

otoko ōna kirawazu yobi-tsudoyete ito kashikoku asobu, and
men and women were invited and assembled, and there was
nought unseemly and full pleasant and full was the revelry.

Notes.

P. 46.

yeteshi gana, miteshi gana !—combinations of p. part. forms
of *uru* (get), *miru* (see), with *shi* (indef. of *su, suru*, do) and
the interjectional word *K(g)ana*—O that (I) might obtain,
O that (I) might see (the Lady Kaguya).

mirumajiki = *mirubekarazu*, may not be seen, invisible.
Majiku(i) is an adjectival form, appended to verbs, like
beku(i), but having an opposite meaning.

yasuki i mo nezu (yasuki-i)—rest-be-even-sleep-not, there
was neither rest nor sleep.

Kaima mi-madoi ayeri should be *Kaima-mi madoi-ayeri*,
ayeri is little more than an auxiliary.

hito no monoshi, etc., should read, according to Daishu, *hito
no mono shi mo senu* = *hitori no hito mo oranu*. The passage
is corrupt; perhaps *monomonoshi* should be read, in which
case the version would run 'they lost all sense of their rank
through their passion.'

Koto to mo sezu—a better reading is *kotaye mo sezu*, made
no answer at all.

ōkari (*ohoku-ari*)—conclus. form of verbalised adj. *ōku* (many). Here, as often in the text, the morphological present is aoristic in value.

yoshinakarikeri=*yoshi-naki-ari-ki-ari* concl. past of neg. adj. verbalised *yoshinaki*, not-good.

nawo iikeru wa—this appears to be a corrupt passage. The general meaning seems to be that of the translation.

kitari keru should read *kikeri*.

da ni—here, as throughout, should read *dani*. Note the use of *wo*.

arubeku mo arazu—be-possible even be-not, *i.e.* was not possible.

arikikeredomo—*ariki-ki-are-to-mo*. This form may be contrasted with *yaredomo*, both are concessive forms, the action being more specialised and momentary in the former than in the latter.

tabe=*tamaye*.

<h1 style="text-align:center">P. 47.</h1>

ono ga—one's own, *i.e.* the Bamboo-Hewer's.

inori oshi should read *inori wo shi*.

guwan (Chinese)—願 is said to be more correct than the pure Japanese *negai*.

henguye (*henge*, Chinese) *no mono nite haberikemu mi to* . . . —the whole phrase up to *mi* (self) qualifies that word.

kyō to mo asu to mo—ellipsis of *shinuran* (may die) after each member of the phrase.

mi-mochi tamayeri should read *mi mochitamayeri kabakari* —the following comma should be deleted.

koso amere (*arame-are*)—verily seem to be.

hitoshi kannari seems to mean 'are all pretty much alike.' The phrase is sometimes allotted to the Hewer, not, as in the translation, to the Lady.

Katajikenaku mo . . .—this involved passage should be dissected out by the student of Japanese. In the text it is wrongly punctuated and should run thus—" *Katajikenaku mo kitanagenaru tokoro ni, toshi tsuki wo hete, mono shitamō koto kiwamaritaru kashikomari* " *to* (*okina*) *mōsu.* Then the

Hewer reports the conversation he has just had with Kaguya. "'*Okina no inochi kyō asu to mo shiranu*' *wo* (*kikite*) *kaku* (*Kaguya*) *notamō*, '*kimidachi ni mo yoku omoi-sadamete tsuko-matsure*,' *to* (*okina*) *mōseba fukaki no kokoro wo shirade wa* (*aigatashi*) *to namu* (Kaguya) *mōsu*'—*samōsu mo kotowari nari*—'*izure otori-masari owashi-maseneba yukashiki mono mise-tamayeramu ni on kokorozashi no hodo miyubeshi, tsukōmatsuramu koto wa sore ni namu sadamubeki*' *to* (Kaguya) *iu* . . ." The word *owashimaseneba* gives a negative turn to the query 'which is the more excellent? Which is not the superior and which is not the inferior?' The general sense is correctly given on p. 6.

urami mo uramaji—an emphatic phrase, there is no hating with hate (of such a man). So in Hebrew, (שירהשירים,) *yisshāqēniy minnshiyqōth.*

P. 48.

Koto domo—a rare instance of a plural of a noun denoting neither person nor thing.

notamawanu should perhaps be read *notamawamu*.

ikitaru to mo should read *ikitari to mo*.

noshikereba should read *no shikereba*.

hachi no hitakuro ni suzukitaru wo=*hitakuro ni suzukitaru hachi wo*.

owashimashinu to hito . . .—the passage is somewhat obscure; perhaps *Hōrai Tsukushi ye yuki-idete* should be understood before *owashimashinu*.

kama ye should read *Kamahe*.

iritamaitsutsu should read *iretamaitsutsu*.

kayeri ki ni keri—a curiously tautological past—*ki ni ki-ari*.

mairitari should be followed by colon or better full stop.

P. 49.

Kayerazaramashi=*kayeri-arazu-aramu-mashi*, an aggluti-nated negative potential sentence-word ending with the particle *mashi*, indicating likelihood, propriety, etc.

hitotsu no tokoro mo ayashiki tokoro naku ayamatazu—in no particular open to doubt and without error.

to kaku . . . should read *to-kaku misubeki ni arazu*, there should be no talk this way and that, *i.e.* no hesitation.

ware on iye should read *waga* (his) *on iye nagekashige—ge* (*ki*) is an affix giving sense of mood, wise, manner, etc. Note honorific use of causative.

Kotowari ni omō—thought all was as it should be.

ito hoshisa ni should be *itōshisa ni*=*kinodoku ni inaimōsamu* should be *inabimōsamu* (or *inamimōsamu*).

inabimōsanu should be *inabimōsamu*. The sentence, of which the translation is not quite correct, means that Kaguya is disappointed that a thing deemed so hard to obtain and so prized on that account should have been won with such paltry ease—*asamashiku* (*aza-ozo-mashiku*), original meaning shallow, hence paltry, mean, ingloriously easy, etc.

oboyeshikado—a concess. part. auxil. form—*oboye-shiki-to*, *shiki* being past of *shi* (*su suru*). Compare *korosamu to shiki* a few lines further on in the text.

narade—p. part. neg. *naru*.

fune no uchi wo semete miru—all in the ship gazed earnestly (*semete*), *wo* is here an emphatic particle.

hona no ki should read *hana no ki*.

kono torite, *kono* is here used for *kore*.

warokarishi ka do should read *warokarishikado*=*waro(u)ku-ari-shiki-to*.

oriteshikaba—a past condit. (not hypothetical) aux. form of *ori*, a verb, break.

daikuwan no chikara ni ya—under pressure, belike (*ya*) of a strong desire.

kitsuru—just arrived.

saya wa should read *sa ya wa*.

P. 50.

Tsuku mo dokoro should read *tsukumo-dokoro*, i.e. *tsukuru mono dokoro*, prepare-thing-place, kitchen. *zukasa* should read *tsukasa, auzuru anzuru, uke tamawatte uketamawatte*.

kikitsureba—cond. past of *kiki* (hear) with aux. *tsuru=tōru.*

takumi ra should read *takumira.*

roku yeshi kai mo naku—their having obtained largesse (wage) turned out of no profit to them.

ye-mi-tsuke-tatematsurazu—get-perceive-did not, *i.e.* could not perceive—a peculiar quasi-passive form used potentially.

sadaijin—Daishu prefers *udaijin.*

minu mono nari—here *minu* is negative.

moshi chōja ni . . . should be rendered 'and if after enquiring among the merchants . . .'

fune kikeri should be followed by a colon, and *hinezumi no Kawagoromo* by a comma.

kashikoki Temujiku no hijiri—*kashikoki* qualifies *hijiri.*

ayumi- tō suru (better *ayumi tō suru*)—*tō* is *toku*, fast, swift.

P. 51.

mime—emph. form of future *mimu*, 'surely shall see shall I not.'

yeshiinu—*ye* with neg. of *shii* (*i* verb), compel, constrain.

yakamu ni yakezuba—in trying to burn it up should it not be burnt up.

sa wa mōsu to mo seems to mean 'such being the case by all means (put it—the fur-robe—to the test of fire). In the paragraph where this sentence occurs are several misprints: for *narame* read *naramu*, *makemu makemu*, *notamō notamaye*, *kokoromite kokoromimu.* For *Daijin* the archaic *otodo* may be read.

shiriseba—a somewhat rare form of cond. past. with aux. *shi (suru).*

Kinezumi should read *hinezumi*, *mera mera-to mera-mera to.*

yake ni shikaba—past cond. form with the two aux. *ni (nu*, be) and *shikaba* cond. past of *shi (suru).*

hime ni sumitamō—be on love-like terms, keep company with, the Lady.

to na—ellipsis for *to (hito ga iu) na*, as men say, do they not.

In the first par. of *Tatsu no kubi* the following misprints occur : *kanawamu* should read *kanayemu*, *one ono*, *notoru noboru*, and *mōsuheki mōsubeki.*

P. 52.

Kimi no na should read *kimi no tsukai to na*—the phrase should be rendered 'are ye not your lord's servants, would ye cast disgrace on the name by opposing his will?'

to notamō should read *to notamaite.*

tote (3rd line) should read *toku.*

hitobito domo (not *hito bito tomo*)—a curious double plural.

kayerikuna—neg. imperat. with aux. *ki* (*ku kuru*).

soshiri-ayeri should be followed by a comma.

Line 10; between *ayeri* and next word insert a hyphen, after *wa dele* comma.

Line 20 *akashi-kurashi-tamō*, a little further on *ochi-kakaru.*

suzuro (not *susuro*), an archaic form of *sozoro.*

umi koto ni . . . should read *umi goto ni* . . . sailing over the sea in all directions.

ikaga shikemu . . . means how it came about none could tell but the wind . . . *shikemu* is a perf. future form of *shi* (*suru*).

kami saye itadaki ni . . . and also the (thunder) god's threatening to hurl down his bolts upon our heads . . . .

16th line from bottom, for *ani* read *nani*, 6th line, for *airazu* read *arazu.*

P. 53.

Line 4, for *tsukasa* read *tsukasa*; *hohoyemitaru* seems ungrammatical, it should be . . . *tari* or . . . *taru nari.*

Line 13, *saru* should read *suru* and *ware* should read *iye.*

Line 17, *no* should intervene between *tsubakurame* and *koyasugai.*

Line 22 from bottom, *tsubakurame no hito* should read *tsub. mo hito.*

Line 10 from top, *sore ga tama* . . . should be rendered 'in essaying to take the dragon-jewel I worked you harm and had I succeeded much more, without doubt, should I have worked harm to my house and 'tis well therefore I did not take it.' A little above *nyōnyō ni nawarete* should read *nyōnyō ninawarete*, 'being borne as he groaned.'

In line 15 *mono domo* is twice used, firstly to signify 'things,' secondly to signify 'persons'—a good example of the want of distinction between persons and things characteristic of Altaic speech.

yuiagete should read *yuite agete.*

Last line, *mōde-koto* should read *mode-ko to.*

P. 54.

Line 8, *shiyetari* is *shi* (do), *yete* (obtained), *ari* (be).

Line 18, *shisokuseshite ko* should read *shisoku sashite maire*, *i.e.* bring a light here; *tsukushi* should read *mi kushi*, the noble (*i.e.* the Chiunagon's) head.

Line 27, *torai* should read *toburai.*

Line 29, *toki* should read *toshi, yaranu yoranu.*

The phrase at bottom, *yo ni sumitamawamu hito no uketa-mawaritamawade wa arinamu ya iwarenu koto*—for one who lives in this world not to listen respectfully (to the royal wish), that such a thing should be, is it not an unspeakable matter?

P. 55.

Koroshitegeru—a not-common verbal form, probably a contraction of *koroshitemu-ki-ari.*

to aritomo kakaritomo, a form of the common phrase *to mo kaku mo.*

shinu beshi, go ranzerare, go ranjitsureba should read *shinubeshi, goranzerare, goranjitsureba.*

umarete haberaba . . . —had she been born in this land she would have been bound to serve Your Majesty.

i (*ite*) is 牽 to drag, take along with. Like *i* 居 to be in a place; it is one of the few *o* verbs.

on moto is the *go sho*, or Palace.

ōserarureba a pleonastic form of the ordinary *ōserareba.*

akazu—neg. of *a* verb *aki*, here meaning to be unsuccessful.

kore wo Mikado goranjite . . . the meaning of the phrase is somewhat obscure; *itodo kayeritamawamu* probably implies the M.'s desire to return to the place where the Lady still abode.

P. 56.

Line 10, *tomo sureba* should read *to mo sureba*=*to mo kaku mo*, i.e. *tokaku*.

aware gari-tamai should read *awaregaritamai*.

umashiki yo ni—*owashimasezaramu ka* is understood.

Line 24, *yuyami* should read *yūyami*.

uchi-ide—i.e. *kotoba*.

komuzu, sarazu—*komu(to)su, saramu (to) su*.

kikoyetarishikado is here little more than an auxiliary attached to *mitsuke*.

take-dachi narabu should read *take tachinarabu*.

tachiwakare, namu, should read *tachiwakarenamu*.

yumizu mo nomarezu—could not swallow even (a cup of) water, warm or cold, *i.e.* choked with distress.

P. 57.

roku ye no tsukasa—the captains of the six companies of Guards (with their commands). These were *sa* and *u* (left and right) *konyefu* (inner Guards) ; *sa* and *u ye mon* (gate Guards) : and *sa* and *u hyōyefu* (military, perhaps one might say, line Guards). These appellations, especially *yemon* and *hyōye*, are still not uncommon elements of personal names, as 'Butler,' 'Vavasour,' 'Stewart,' are with us.

Line 11, *moya no uchi* should read *mo ya* . . .

Line 21, 22, *koba kinaba*—hypothetical forms of *o* verb. *ki (kuru)*, the latter with *ni (naru)* as auxiliary.

sagashiri, sagakami are believed to be archaisms for *sore ya (shiri, kami)*.

kaki-idete-kokora should read *kaki-idete kokora*.

ima sukarizuru should read *imazukaritsuru*=*tsukōmatsuru*.

Line 29, *omōga oya tachi* should read *omō ga, oyatachi*.

imijiku mo haberazu—is not a weighty matter, is not what I very much desire, or desire at all.

in to suredomo—*in* is *imu*, fut. *i*, aim, shoot at.

Miyakko-Maro môde-ko should be within inverted commas.

11th line from bottom, *iwaku* has the Archangel for subject.

Line 24 from bottom, for *mune idaki* read *mune itaki*, the version should be 'the Ancient, sad at heart, said "do not so, beings of form so lovely may not be hindered;"' for *urawashiki* read *uruwashiki*, line 23 for *yohi* read *yoi*.

Line 16 from bottom, *kikereba* past cond. *kike* having here sense of taking effect in, attaining.

shire ni shirete, emphatic locution for *shirete*.

sōzoku = shōzoku, raiment.

naki-nageku atawanu koto nari—to weep and lament is improper, unreasonable, not what should be.

P. 58.

to ii-tate kometaru . . . should read *to iu. Tate-kometaru* . . .

koko ni mo is equivalent to *waga mi*, i.e. *Kaguya.* Line 8, *madoinu* should be followed by a full stop, and from *fumi wo kaki* to *mi-tamaye* should be within inverted commas.

kono kuni ni umarenuru . . . the version should be "had I been born in this land (on earth) I should not thus grieve you by my departure, but now, on the contrary, must an intolerable wretchedness be endured. I doff my mantle, and leave it with you as a relic, and when the moon lights up the night may my father send his glance skywards, and though his eyes will vainly search the heavens for me, I shall yet yearn to descend upon earth to stand once more in his gaze."

Line 29, *kokoro ni tomari*—stays in, *i.e.* weighs upon, my heart.

Line 31, *tō no chiushō*—Takano is meant, previously, by mistake probably, called *shōshō*; line 44, *yama, namu* should read *yama namu*—*namu* is fut. of *ni (naru)*, be in, at, etc.

Line 41, *kikoshimesezu* here means 'ate not,' 'took no food.'

nani ni ka wa semu—shall I make anything of it?—*ka wa* implies the answer No, like the Latin 'num.'

VOCABULARY.

Sinico-Japanese words are marked (Ch.).

Only the archaic meanings necessary for the comprehension of the text are, as a rule, given.[1]

Abe, family name of one of the Suitors. Originally, probably, a place-name ; *-be*=Ainu *pet,* stream.

abenashi. See note, p. 19, *ayenashi.*

ada, vain, false, fickle.

aga, for *waga,* mine.

age-suye, v.t. lift-pose ; *-raretari* = were raised up and placed in.

agura, a sort of scaffolding or platform ; *age-gura* (*kura* = seat).

ai- (*au-ō*), *a* vb., meet; prefixed to verbs, etc., gives idea of mutuality.

　　ai-tatakau, fight together.

airazu, misprint for *arazu* (*ari*).

akari, a vb., grow light (ruddy), clear up.

akasa, redness. See *akashi.*

akashi, lit. make open (causat. of *aki*); hence, make open night to dawn, ruddiness of dawn.

akashi, kurashi tamau, wait for dawn and wait for dusk, *i.e.* passed the days and nights.

akazu, neg. of *a* verbs *aki,* have enough of, and *aki,* be open.

ake (*ru, te*), *e* verb, open, dawn.

akegure, dawn and dusk, whole day.

aki, a vb., *aki ni akinu,* be open, open.

akinai, trade, commerce.

akinamu, au aux. fut. form of *aki,* q.v.

Akita, one of the names of Kaguya.

Ama, Heaven, sky; *-bito,* celestial being, angel.

ame=*ama, ame no shita*=*tenka* (Ch. *t'ien-hia*), under-heaven, the empire, the world; also, rain, but not in the text.

amata, many, numerous.

amarinu, part. concl. *a* vb. *amari,* be in excess, abundant.

amere=*aramu-are.*

ana, an interjection of surprise, etc. See p. 24.

ana, a hole.

---

[1] The compiler could not obtain Dr. Hepburn's third edition of his admirable Dictionary in time to use it in the preparation of this Vocabulary.

anagachi ni, said to=*mushō ni*, perhaps best rendered in text (p. 47) persistently, obstinately.

ananai, scaffold or platform; *ashijiro*.

anare=*ari-nare*=*ari-ni-are*.

anaru=*arinaru*.

anata (*ano kata*), that quarter, that person (mod. you).

ani, *interrogational interjection* implying negative answer, like 'num.'

annari=*ari-nari*.

anzuru (*anji*), ponder, reflect, Chinese 安 verbalised.

aohedo, green spittle, bilious matter of vomit.

arako, panier, basket, cage.

aramu, fut. of *ari*, q.v.

aranu, neg. of *ari*, q.v.

arazarishi (*aranu-su-ari-shi*), att. past neg. *ari*, q.v.

arazu=*aranu*, q.v.

are, *e* vb., be rough, stormy, rage, toss, wild, etc.

are, emphatic form of *ari*, has sense of completion, hence of past time.

ari, concl. form of *aru*, be, exist, have; *arubeku*, *beki*, *majiki*, *keri*, *kedomo*, *te*, *tsuru*, etc.

ariki, *a* vb., walk, pace about.

arisama, condition, state.

aruiwa, and again, or.

aruji, lord, master (*aru-nushi*).

asa, morning.

asamashigari, be struck of a heap (with wonder, etc.). See next.

asamashiku (*azam.*), said to mean

akireru; *ozomashiku*, etc., here probably implies strangeness, wonderfulness, etc.

ashiki (*ku*), evil, bad; *-karamu*, will or may be bad, etc.

ashitori, foot-take, take by foot, pull out by feet.

asobi, divert oneself, do; sometimes an honorific aux.

asu, to-morrow.

atai, price; *atai*, a vb. (*ata*[*w-y*]-*i*), be proper, able, equal to, etc.

atari, neighbourhood.

atawanu, neg. of *atai*, q.v.

atenaru, of gentle birth; *ate* is supposed to be a contraction of *uwate*, 手上=品上.

ateyaka ni, elegantly, agreeably.

atsumarinu, past form of *a* vb. (*atsumari*), gather together, assemble.

atsumete, p.part. (*atsume*), bring together, collect.

au. See *ai*.

auge (*ōgi*), *a* vb., look up to suppliantwise, entreat.

auzuru is a misprint for *anzuru*, q.v.

awamu, fut. of *ai* (*awi*); *awan*= *awamu*.

aware, excl. of pity, compassion; *aware to mite oru ni*, p. 49; *-gari*, pitiable; *-garase*, cause to be pitiable, etc.

awasemu, fut. of caus. of (*ai awi*), *awasezaramu*, fut. neg. of caus. of *ai* (*awi*).

awatenu, not losing composure, not to be excited.

awazanaru, attr. neg., with aux. *naru*, of *ai* (*awi*).

aya, a sort of figured silk fabric.

Ayabe, prop. name.

ayamatazu, neg. of *ayamachi*, err, fail.

ayashi (*gari*), be astonished at; *-ki*, strange, wonderful.

aye, emphatic form of *ai* (*awi* or *ayi*).

ayeri, past of *ai* (*awi* or *ayi*).

ayeba, conditional of *ai* (*awi* or *ayi*).

ayōsa, dangerousness, perilousness.

ayumi· tō, should be *ayumi tō*; *tō* is *toku*, swift.

ayumi, a vb., walk, march; *ayumi tō suru muma* (p. 50), a swiftly going horse.

azukari, place under charge of; *hito ni mono wo.*

ba, form of postposition *wa*, q.v.; in compos. and after *wo*. See p. 69.

bakari, only, not more than, just.

ban (Ch.), watch, guard.

be, a collective suffix, *kami-dachi-be.*

Binzuru, a Budd. deity. See p. 8.

chichi, father.

chigiri, relation(person to person), intercourse, compact.

chigo, child.

chigusa, thousand herbs, all green things, all sorts of, etc.

chikaki, att. adj., near.

chikara, strength.

chitabi, thousand times.

Chiunagon (Ch.), name of an officer of high rank at Mikado's court, councillor of state.

chiushō (Ch.), middle commander (Lieut.-Gen.); *tō no*, Senior Lieut.-Gen.

chō (Ch.) 帳, curtain. See p. 81.

chō, contraction for *to iu*; *Kito iu hito*, the creature they call K.

chōja (Ch.), elders, in the text = " senior (and wealthier) merchants."

chokushi (Ch.), imperial order.

chōzesase (*chō* is Ch.), punish, cause to be punished.

dachi=tachi, a plural suffix.

dai (Ch.), great; *-kuwan* (or *guwan*), great petition, great desire; *-jin* (Ch.), see *otodo*; *-nagon* (Ch.), office next in rank above a *Chiunagon.*

dani, even, indeed. (Misprinted in text *da ni.*)

dashi, caus. of *de.*

de=ide, go or come forth.

domo, a plural suffix.

domo (*to mo*), concessive particle, though, even if, etc.

fubasami, letter-clipping bamboo staff, bamboo with cleft to hold petition.

Fuji, name of the mountain known to foreigners as Fusiyama.

fukaki, att. adj., deep, profound.

fukare, quasi pass. *fuki*, blow.

fukase, caus. of *fuki*, blow.

fuke, laten, vb. int.

fuki, indef. *a* vb., blow; *-yoserare*, be blow-driven to ; *-kayeshi*, blow back ; *-mawashi*, blow round, about.

fukure, be swollen.

fukuro, bag.

fumi, a writing, letter ; the Chinese 文 assimilated.

fune, boat.

funabito (*funebito*), sailor.

funazoko (*fune soko*), bottom, hold of boat.

furi, a vb., shower down.

furu, att. of *furi;* also, as in text, an adject. root, old, ancient.

fushi, fall prostrate.

fushi, internode of a bamboo.

fushi ogami, fall down in prayer.

futatsu, two.

futabito, two persons.

futagi, a vb., in text, cover, stop from view (face).

futo, suddenly.

futsu, two.

fu-tsuki, full moon (*futo-tsuki*); also seventh month (month of harvest moon).

fuye, flute.

gai (Ch.), 害 harm, injure.

gana. See *kana*.

ge ni, verily, indeed.

gisu. See *kisu*.

go (Ch.), five; *gojiu*, fifty.

go-ran (Ch.), verbalised by *su*, etc., to see, look ; *go* is honorific.

goto ni, asa goto, yū goto ni, morning after morning, evening after evening.

gotoku, suspensive adj., like, thus being.

gushi (*gu* Ch.), accompany.

guwan (Ch.), desire, petition.

ha, eight.

ha, feather.

haberazameri, conclus. neg. dub. form with double auxil. from *haberi=* would seem not to be.

haberi, honorific auxiliary suffixed to verbs; *haberanu, -ru, -rikemu, -ritsuru*, etc.

hachi, bowl.

hafu, gable end, roof.

hageshi(*ku*), violent.

hagoromo, feather-robe.

haha, mother.

hai-nobori, creep-ascend.

haji, shame ; *haji-mise*, put to, show up to, shame.

hajime, begin, beginning.

hajishiku, ashamed.

hakanaku, for a brief time, fleeting ; *hakanaku kuchioshiu to oboshite*, feeling that it was (the vision) briefly sad, i.e. regrettably brief.

hako, box, coffer.

hama, shore.

hanachi, a vb., let loose, let go, utter.

hanare, be separate, apart, aloof from.

hara, belly.

haradatashiki, angry, displeased, lit. belly-setting-up.

hari, a vb., stretch, spread, *orimono . . . ma goto ni hari-tari*, hung every chamber with woven stuffs.

Harima, name of province.

haru, spring (season).

hasami, a vb., clip, hold between.

hashiri, a vb., run.

hashita; *tatsu mo hashita iru mo hashita*, hesitating whether to depart or to go in; *hashita* seems to imply defectiveness.

hata; *-tose*, twenty years.

hate, e vb., end, cease.

hatsuki, eighth month.

hatsuru. See *hate*.

haya, adj. root (*hayaki*, etc.), early, quick, also used as exclamation = Lat. 'agedum.'

hayate, storm.

hazukashi, feeling ashamed.

hedate, e vb., separate, split.

henguye (Ch), transformation; in mod. Japanese *henge* 化變.

henji (Ch.), answer.

he, e vb., pass through and away (time), etc.

henuru, a past form of *he*.

hete, p.part. *he*.

hi, sun, day, fire.

higashi(*hi mukashi*),sun-towards, i.e. east.

hige, beard, face-hair.

higoro, day by day, daily, usual.

higure, day- or sun-darken, dusk, grow dusk.

hijiri, priest (Buddh.).

hikari, light, radiance, brightness.

hikari-michi (*mitsu*), be full of light, brightness.

hikaru, a verb, be shining, radiant.

hikiage, draw-lift, draw up.

hikigushi (*gu* is Ch.), accompany, with sense of bringing along, French 'emmener.'

hikisugi, pass, go beyond, in the sense of bringing along.

hima, space, interval, chink; later, leisure.

hime, lady, princess.

hi-nezumi, fire-rat, salamander.

hirame, make flat.

hirameki, a vb., toss up and down, glitter, flash.

hiroge, e vb., open out, unroll.

hiroki, attributive adj., broad, spacious.

hiru, day time.

hisashiku, suspensive adj., long (in time).

hitaburu (perhaps *hitai-furu*, brow-shake); with *ni* persistently.

hitai, forehead.

hitakuro (*hita kuro*), deep black, quite black.

hito, one, being, man, person; *hitobito*, men, persons; *hitotsu*, one.

hitogiki (man-hear), publicity, the becoming matter of public gossip, etc.

hitoma, man-space, i.e. void of men, solitary or empty place or chamber. Perhaps simply 一 閒.

hitori, one person, alone; *hitori-bitori ni*, one (person) after the other.

hitoshi, simple, equal, like.

ho. See *ho i naku*.

hō (*kata*), quarter, direction.

hodo, quantity, space, measure, fullness; *tsuki no hodo ni*, as the moon waxed; *hodonaku*, at once.

hohoyemi, a vb.(?), smile, laugh.

ho-i-naku (*hon-i*, Ch.), against one's will or desire.

Hokanruri, prop. name of Buddhist origin. In some texts *Hokamu*.

hokazama, otherwise - fashion method appearance; astray.

Hōrai (Ch.), name of fabulous mountain (P'êng-lai).

hoshisa, desiringness, desire.

hotaru, firefly.

hotoke, Buddha, also darling, precious.

hyaku (Ch.), one hundred; *hyaku-kwan*. See p. 27.

i, take along with, be in or at, be.

ichi (Ch.), one, whole, altogether.

idakaye. See *idaki*.

idaki, embrace, hold to one, etc. (not as a salutation).

idasazu, neg. caus. *ide*.

ide (*izuru*), go, come forth ; in compos. denotes motion as Germ. 'hin' and 'her.'

   ide-ai, go-forth-meet, meet by mutual going forth.

   ide-i, come-forth-be, come or go to and be in a place, etc.

   ide-ki, come-forth-come, come from.

   ide-soye, emphatic of *ide-soi* (or quasi-pass.).

iho, five hundred; mod. *go hiyaku*.

iho, house, dwelling, cabin.

ii (*iwi, iyi, iu*), *a* vb., say, speak, call ; *iyeru*, att. past form.

   ii-hajime, begin to say.

   ii-itari, was saying, said.

   ii-kakare, speak to or with.

   ii-oki, say - place, direct, order.

   ii-tate, declare, announce.

   ii-tsutaye, hand down orally.

   ii-wazurai, get sick of talking.

ii 飯, boiled rice.

ika, how.

   ikabakari, how much.

   ikade, how.

   ikadeka, howsoever.

   ikaga, how.

   ikanaru, what ?

   ikayō, what kind ?

ikameshiu, dignifiedly.

iki. See *yuki*.

ikioi, power, influence, weight ; lit. breath (life) abundant.

iki-tsuki, a vb. (comp.), breath-stick, catch breath (with fright, etc.).

i-koroshi (*i-korosu*), aim-kill, aim at and kill.

ima, now, present moment.

imada, not yet (always with neg. vb.).

imasara, now at all events.

imashi, a vb., be, be at, dwell in.

imazu = *ima zo*.

imasukari imashi, q.v., *owashi-masu*, nearly. Note 3, p. 47, should be deleted.

imi, a vb., feel sad, dislike, shun.

imijiku, adj., exceeding, intense, firm, severe.

imo-i, seclusion, withdrawal from social life, pleasures, etc., for purification, connected with *imi*, *a* vb., shun.

imu, fut. of *i*, aim at.

Imube, prop. name. See p. 2, note 3.

in. See *imu*.

ina, no.

inabi. See *inami*.

inami, a vb., refuse.

inamu, *inan*, fut., *ini*, *a* vb., go away.

inochi, life.

inori, pray.

inu, *inuru*, past forms of *ini*. See *inamu*.

irayuru, a peculiar form deriv. probably of *ii*, say, reply, answer.

irazuba, neg., hypothetical of *iri*, enter, etc.

ire, *e* vb., put in, trans. of *iri*.

irete, p.part. *ire*.

iri (*iru*, *irite*), enter, go in.

irogonomi, love, passion.

iroiro, different kinds of, various (with *no*=adj.).

iroye, *e* vb. = *irodori*, colour, adorn with colours; *iroye-shi*, the same verbalised causatively.

isasaka, petty, scant, small.

ishi, stone.

iso, rock.

isoji, fifty (years old).

isshō (Ch.), through life, life-long.

itadaki, top, summit, head.

itaku-shite, taking pains, taking trouble.

itari, rush to, arrive at.

itazura (*ita-tsura*, pain-face); with *ni*, dolorously, ruinously, (later) vainly; *ni nasu*, to harm, ruin.

ite, p. part. of *i*, take along with; *ite-ikaji*=*ite yukaji*; *yukaji* is concl. neg. fut. of *yuku*, go.

ito, *itō*, very, exceeding, with pains.

itodo, *ito*, q.v.

itōma, with *mōsu*, take leave.

itsuka, any time, some time; *itsuka kikemu* (p. 48), will at any time whatever be heard of, i.e. famous.

itsuki-kashizuki, attend upon and cherish.

iu. See *ii*.

iuramu, a future form of *ii*.

iwaku, form of *iu*, say, used only to introduce quoted words.

iwamu. See *ii*.

iwanya, lit. 'num dicendum?' much more, rather.

iwaruru, quasi-pass. form of *ii*.

iwase, causat. (honorific) form of *ii*.

iyashiki, att. adj., low, mean, base.

iye, *i-he*=be-place, i.e. residence, dwelling.

iyeru, past. att. of *ii*, q.v.

iza, Ho! there.

izuchi, where?

izure, which, what, who?

jiuroku (Ch.), sixteen.

ka, interr. and dubit. particle, often gives indefinite sense to interrogative pronouns.

ka, a day; *nanuka*, seven days.

kabakari, kaku bakari, thus much, just so much.

kado, house, door, corner.

kagamari, a vb., be crooked, bent.

kagawari, should be *kagamari*, q.v.

kagayaki, sparkle, gleam.

kage, shade, shadow.

kagiri, end, limit, termination; *-nashi*, boundless.

Kaguya, prop. name.

kai (Ch.), 斐 甲 ; *-nashi*, useless, vain; also 貝, a shell.

kaima-mi. See p. 82.

kajitori, steersman.

kakareba, kaku areba, p. 47.

kakaye, get hold of, clutch, hold fast.

kake, e vb., suspend, put to, etc., *tanomi wo kaketari*, continued proffering their suit.

kaki, write.

kaki, fence, hedge.

kaki-ide, scratch out, claw to pieces.

kaku, thus.

kakumare, kaku mo are.

kakure, hide, conceal oneself, get hidden, etc.

kakushi, hide, conceal (vb. trans.).

kakute, thus it was and . . . See *kaku.*

kamaye, fit to, adapt to.

kami, lord, god; also *kami*, hair (*kami-age*. See pp. 2, 81).

kaminari, thunder, lit. God's roar.

kana, interjection, implying longing or regret or admiration.

kanaguri-otoshi, a vb. (comp.), twist or screw out of.

kanai, a vb. (*kana-w-y-i*), be in accordance with; *negai wo*, obtain desire.

kanamaru, metal bowl or jar.

kanarazu, gives idea of necessity to sequent verb.

kanashi, wretched.

kanaye, quasi-passive of *kanai*, q.v. (or stem-form).

kanaye, cauldron.

kanawamu, fut. of *kanai*, q.v.

kandō (Ch.), 當 勘 expulsion from clan or household.

kane, metal, copper, bronze.

kanete, previously.

kanōru, att. and concl. form of *kanai*, q.v.

kannari＝ka nari, be average in quality, etc.

kao, face, visage.

karabitsu (*bitsu* is Ch., *kara*, perhaps＝*kōrai*, korea, Ch. *kao-li*), a leather box, lit. China box.

kari, hunt.

kare, that, he, it, etc.

karōjite, hardly, painfully, laboriously; *karaku*(ō), pungent, hard, disagreeable, verbalised with *shi.*

kasanari, a vb., accumulate (intransitive).

kasanarinu, past form of *kasanari.*

kashi, a final particle, giving emphasis or notion of entreaty, etc., to verb.

kashiki (*kashiku*), cook rice.

kashiko, there.

kashikomaru, humilific verb, more or less auxiliary＝your servant obeys.

kashira, head, chief.

kata, quarter, direction, position.

katabuki, *a* vb., same as *katamuki*, bend or lean aside.

katachi, form, shape.

katagata, pl. of *kata*, quarter, place, side, person.

katajikenaku, grateful, thankful.

kataki, enemy.

katami, memorial gift, souvenir.

katarai, chat, talk, say.

katatoki, for a while, for a time.

katawara, side.

kate, victuals.

kawa, skin, fur.

kawa, river, stream.

kawaki, dry up, become dry.

kawahori, bat (animal).

kayeri (*kaye-ari?*), return, vb. intrans.

kayeshi, caus. *a* vb. trans., return, give back.

kayesugayesu, over and over again.

kayowasase, causat. of *kayo(w)i*; hence, to make go, move, etc., to and fro, thence and back, etc.

kazareru, att. past *kazari*, adorn.

kaze, wind, cold in head.

kazu, sum, total, amount, number.

kazuke, *e* vb., bestow, give to, given in charge of.

ke, hair, fur.

keburi, smoke (*kemuri*).

kego (*ka-ko*, hybrid compd.), family = *iye no ko*.

keri (*ki-ari*), auxil. past form.

keshiki (Ch.), appearance, expression.

kesō = keshō (Ch.), face-powder.

ki, tree.

ki-gusa, tree (and) herb.

kikase, caus. *e* vb., cause to listen, inform, etc.

kike, emphat. form of *kiki*, q.v.

kiki, *a* vb., listen, hear, etc. Its original meaning seems to have been the attaining or producing effect. Perhaps it is an emphatic duplication of *ki* (*ko, kuru*), expressing motion to or from a place; *hokazama ye kikereba*, as (the arrow) flew (took effect) astray (from its mark).

kikoshimeshi, an honorific causative of *kiki*, to hear (i.e. causing oneself to be made to hear); on p. 58 it means to partake of food or drink; often a mere honorific auxiliary.

kikoye, quasi-pass. *kiki*, to get heard of, be known, famous, etc., sometimes a mere honorific aux. as on p. 56, *mitsuke-kikoyetarishikaba*, also *mukaye-kikoyemu, asobi-kikoyete.*

kikoye kawashi, interchange communication, exchange correspondence.

kimi, lord, mistress.

kimo, liver (jœur).

kinō, yesterday.

kinu, past of *ki*, come, go.

kinu, silk fabric.

kirawazu, neg. of *kirai* (*kirawi*, *a* vb.), dislike.

kiri, *a* vb., cut; *hara-kiri-warai*, cut-belly-laugh, i.e. laugh consumedly, split one's sides with laughter.

kirite, p.part. *kiri.*

kiru, a vb., see *kiri*; *kiru, i* vb. (*ki-kiru*), put on (clothes), don.

kisaragi, name of second month.

kise, trans. of *i* vb. *kiru*, put on.

kitanage-naru, foul, unclean, adj. root with *naru*, be.

kitanaki, att. adj. unclean, soiled.

kito, all at once, suddenly.

kiwamari, settle, fix, decide.

kiye, e vb., vanish, fade away.

kiyōra (with *naru*), clean, pure, clear, apparently an emphatic form of *kiyoki*.

ko, child.

ko, bamboo basket.

kō (*kaku*), thus.

kobochi, a vb. (*kobotsu*), shatter, break.

kochi, here, hither.

kogane, gold.

kogi, i vb.(?), scull, row.

koishikari (*koishiki-ari*), beloved, be object of fondness, affection.

koko, here, in this place.

kokochi, condition of spirits, 'gemuth.'

kokoro, heart, will, intention; *-baye*, disposition; *-gurushiku*, heart-oppressed, wretched; *-bosoku* (*hosoku*), heart-thin, feeble, wretched.

kokushi (Ch.), governor of province.

komagoma, minutely, fully, in detail.

kome, rice (unboiled but cleaned).

kome, e vb., confine, inclose, shut up in.

komori, be shut up in.

komu zu=*komu zo*; *komu* (*kon*) is fut. of *o* verb (*ki, kuru*), come.

konata, kono kata.

konomoshikari, adj. with aux. *ari*, desirable.

konu, att. neg. *o* vb. (*ki kuru*), come.

kōri, a land-division next in size to province.

koro, time, period.

koromo, garment.

koroshi, a vb., kill.

kōshi (Ch.), lattice, lattice-work.

koso, emph. dissyllabic particle, used generally with emph. verbal form in *e*.

kōte, kakute.

koto, affair, thing, 'res'; added to verbs and adjectives, concretes act or quality.

koto, different, extraordinary; *koto mo naku*, as a matter of course; *koto mono*, counterfeit.

kotoba, language, speech, word.

kotoshi, this year; *kono toshi*.

kotowari, reason, foundation in reason, reasonableness, etc., 理.

kotaye, e vb., answer.

kowadakani, loudly (*koye-taka*).

kowaku, unpliable, stiff, indocile, difficult to influence.

koyasugai, a kind of cowry shell. See p. 38.

koyuru, att. form, pass over, on towards.

kozu, neg. of *ki* (*kuru*), come.

kubi, neck.

kubete (*kube*), *e* vb., cast in (the fire).

kuchi, mouth, entrance.

kuchioshiku, regrettable, pitiable.

kudari, a vb., descend (said of coming *down* from the capital). Not used honorifically (as in mod. Jap.) in the text.

kudaki, a vb., break in pieces, shatter.

kudo, furnace, oven (for pottery).

kudoku (Ch.), righteousness, merit obtained by pious life (Buddhist term).

kui, a vb., chew, eat; *su wo kui*, build nest.

kujiri, a vb., bore.

kuki, stalk, stem.

kumi, draw water.

kumo, cloud.

kuni, country, province.

kuragari, grow dark.

kuraki, att. adj., dark, gloomy.

Kuramochi, name of the second suitor.

kurashi, a vb., *hi wo k.*, see day through up to dusk.

Kuratsumaro, name of a retainer of the fifth suitor.

kurenureba, past cond. *kure*, set, go down (sun), darken.

kuretake, a kind of bamboo (*take*), perhaps a reddish hued (*kure*) one.

kururu, e vb., be gloomy, dark.

kurushige, wretchedness, distress-ingness.

kusa, herb, grass; *kusa-gusa*, all sorts of.

kushi = kashira, head.

kuso, dung.

kusuri, drug, physic.

kuwan-nin (Ch.), official, palace-servant or retainer.

kuwaye, add on, join.

kuwazu, neg. of *a* vb., *ku(wo)i*, eat.

kyō (Ch.), to-day.

kyō (Ch.), diversion, amusement 興.

ma, space (tract of time or place).

ma, chamber; *ma goto ni*, each chamber, chamber by chamber.

machi, a vb., wait, expect.

made, until, up to.

madoi, a vb., (*mado-w-y-i*), be distracted, confused.

magire, e vb., be confused with, lost in.

mairi, a vb., go, come.

majiri, a vb., mingle with or to-gether; *yama ni majirite*, lost himself among the hills and . . .

makari, a vb., go down, go; often a sort of auxiliary embellish-ment. See Chamberlain's Grammar.

makase, confide to, entrust with (*hito ni mono wo*).

make, yield, draw back from.

maki-ire, e vb. (comp.), roll over into.

makiye, lacquer ornamented with gold and silver designs.

makoto, true.

mama, state, condition.

mame, *mame naru hito*, men on watch or guard.

mamorasu, causat. of *mamori*.

mamori, guard, protect, keep watch.

man (Ch.) = *ban*, ten thousand.

manako, pupil of eye, eye.

mari-okeru, roll up and deposit, deposit in a rounded form.

Marotada, prop. name.

masa, *masa ni*, just, exactly, properly ; *masa-nashi*, improper, wrong, ἀεικής.

mashi, a particle affixed to concl. form of verbs, implying that the action was expected, but has not taken place. See p. 48, *yadosumashi*; but this may be a conclusive form of the neg. pot. *yadosumajiki*.

mashite, p.part. *mashi*, increase ; in the text the word means yet more, much more.

mataji, fut. neg. *machi*, wait, expect.

matsu. See *machi*.

matsu, pine-tree.

maye, before (time and place).

mazu, first of all, just, at once.

me, female, woman, wife.

me, eye.

me, particle added to adjectives having something like force of -ness, -hood, etc. ; thus, *wabishiki-me* = wretchedness, wretched condition.

medetaki, att. adj., lovely.

medete, p.part. *e* vb., *mede*, love.

megurashi, caus. *meguri*, q.v.

meguri, a vb., go round, make circuit of.

mera-mera, *mera mera to yake*, in a crackling manner, shrivelling and being consumed in a flash.

meshite, p.part. *a* vb. *meshi*, summon, send for.

meshitori, comp. vb., seize, arrest.

meshitsugi, convey or send orders to.

mi, fruit.

mi, three.

mi, self, person, body, form.

mi, look, see, attrib. form *miru*.

mi, honorific prefix to nouns. Used with what appertains to Mikado, but in one instance, p. 52, *mi mushiro*, with what is merely official, and, p. 54, *mi kushi*, with what is not even official.

michi, path, way.

michi, a vb. (*mitsu*), be full of.

mide, p.part. neg. *mi*, see.

miji, fut. neg. of *mi*, see.

Mikado, the Emperor, almost lit. 'Sublime Porte.'

mikari, state-hunt.

mikoto, imperial command, message.

mimahoshi(k)u, desirous to see.

mi-madoi, comp. vb., see and be confused, distracted, dazzled, etc.

mimashi, would see.

mime, emphatic of fut. form of *mi*, see ; *kiyō koso wa mime*, to-day shall I surely see her.

mimi, ear.

mimu (*min*), fut. *mi*, see.

Mimuro, one of the names of Kaguya.

mina, all, whole.

minarai = *mi-nare*, be accustomed to see.

mine, top, summit, peak.

mi-nikushi, see-disagreeable, ugly.

mi-okose, send glance, look at.

mi-okuri, accompany with eyes, watch one going away.

mireba, cond. form of *mi*.

miru. See *mi*.

mise, caus. of *mi*.

misoka, thirtieth day, last day of month.

misu, roll-blind or screen of fine bamboo-strips.

miteshi. See p. 82.

mitsu, three (*tsu* is old generic part. attached to *mi*).

mitsuke, *e* vb., catch sight of, look at.

mitsukuru, attrib. form of *mitsuke*.

Miushi, name of third suitor.

mi-warai, see-laugh, see and laugh at.

miya, shrine, palace.

miyako, royal or imperial residence, city.

Miyakko. See p. 1, note.

Miyazukaye, palace servant, lady in attendance on Mikado.

miyu, conclus. form of quasi-pass. of *mi*, see, be seen, visible, etc.

mi-yuki, a progress or going forth of the Mikado.

mizu, neg. *mi*, see.

mizu, water.

mo, also, even; a concessive and hypothetical particle.

mo, a gown anciently worn by girls on attaining maidenhood.

mō (Ch.) See *ikioi mō*, p. 82.

mochi (*motsu*), *a* vb., have, hold, grasp, take.

mochi, full moon.

mōde, *e* vb. See *mōdeki*.

mōdeki, *i* vb., come or go forth, usually to pay a visit complimentary or other.

mōde-toburai, come to make respectful inquiry of.

mo-gi-su = *mo wo ki suru*, cause to don the robe of . . .

mohara, *moppara*, with neg. vb. = in no case, not at all, οὐκ ἔμπης.

mōkeshite = *mōke*, *e* vb. (p. 52, strive after 'and obtain), with aux. *shi*, do.

mono, thing, person.

mononofu, men-at-arms.

monoshi. See p. 82.

Morokoshi, China.

morotomo ni, all together, together.

mōsaku, a form of *mōsu* (*mōshi*). The form in *aku* has no conjugation, and is used to introduce a quotation (Mr. Chamberlain's Grammar, p. 70).

mōshi (*mōsu*), speak, say; sometimes a mere humilific auxil.

moshi, if.

motage, take-lift, raise, lift up.

motaru, *mote aru*. See *mochi*.

mote. See *mochi*.

moto, origin, source; *on moto*, palace; *moto hikaru*, shining of itself.

motome, *e* vb., search after, get.

moya, house place, residential part of house (*omoya*).

mugura, the Japanese hop, *Humulus japonicus*.

mukai, *a* vb. (*muka-w-y-i*), meet, confront, come or go towards (an emphatic form of *muki*).

mukashi, of yore, long ago, formerly.

mukawase, caus. of *mukai*, q.v.

mukaye, an emphatic form of *mukai*, giving, transitive force.

mukayesase, caus. of *mukaye*.

muki, a vb., turn towards, face.

mukitaramu, fut. past *muki*.

mukōru, identical with *mukayeru*?

mukutsuge, properly *mukutsuke-ge*, terrible and loathsome-like.

munashi, empty; *munashiki kaze* might be rendered direction-less or wayless winds.

mune, roof ridge.

mushiro, mat.

musume, girl, maiden.

muya. See *moya*.

na, name.

na, imperat. neg. particle used with final *so*; *na ariki so*, do not walk there.

nado. See p. 62.

nagahitsu, a kind of Chinese trunk or coffer. *Naga* is Japanese, *hitsu* is Chinese.

nagaki, long.

nagara, while, during.

nagare, flow.

nagari (*naga-ari*?) pp. 52 and 58, to be long, over long; *kokoromoto nagari*, 'tis trouble-some, heart-wearying.

nagaruru, attrib. of *nagare*.

nagashitsu, past of *nagashi*, throw away.

nageki, a vb., grieve, lament, be sorrowful.

nagekashige. See *nageki*, also p. 61.

nagori, vestige, remains.

naishi (Ch.), ladies in waiting on the Mikado.

najō, a contraction of *nani to iu*.

naka, inside.

naka ni, in middle of, in, etc.

nakari, neg. adject. *naku*, verbal-ised with *ari*.

Nakatomi no Fusako, name of Naishi sent to report on beauty of Kaguya.

naki (*naku*), a vb., weep, cry, scream out.

naki-fuse, e vb., lie prostrate weeping on ground.

naki-nonoshiri, a vb., while weep-ing to shout, abuse, etc.

naku, suspensive adj. (*naki*, *nashi*), lacking, not-being.

naku-naku, weep-weep, to weep and weep, keep weeping.

namashi, a vb., *ni* (be) with part. *mashi*.

namege, ill-bred, vulgar, raw.

nameri, perhaps *namu* (fut. of *ni*, be)+*ari*, will, must, should, may be taken to be.

namida, tears.

namu(*n*), fut. of *ni* (*naru*) be; almost=Germ. *doch*.

namuji. See *namujira*.

namujira=*nanjira*, plur. of *nanji*, you (said to=*na-mochi*, name-possessor). Compare Span. 'hidalgo.'

nan. See *namu*.

nanasoji, seventy years of age.

nanatabi, seven times.

nani, what? *nani ka*, anything, something or other.

Naniwa, ancient name of Ozaka.

nanji. See *namuji*.

nanjira. See *namujira*.

nan-kai (Ch.), southern seas.

nanuka (*nanoka*), seven days.

narabi-nashi, incomparable.

narade, neg. p.part. *nari*.

narai, a vb., on p. 56 seems to have force of *nare*, grow accustomed to.

narame, emphatic form of future of *nari*.

narashi, causat. of *nari*, to sound.

narawashi, a vb., caus. of *narai*, learn.

nari, a closing verb having little more than the value of a full stop. See also *naru*.

nari-masaru, become, increase, i.e. grew and grew.

nari-yuku, with *ni* preceding, go on becoming . . .

naru (*ni-aru*), be ; preceded by p.position *ni*=become ; added to adjectiv. roots forms attr. adjectives.

nasanu, neg. of *nashi* (*nasu*), causat. of *ni*.

nashi. See *naku*.

natane, the seed of the rape brassica.

naye-kagamari, a vb. (compound), be cramped, paralysed.

Nayotake, graceful bamboo, one of the names of Kaguya.

nazukeru, name, bestow name on.

ne, root.

neburi, a vb., in the text, p. 50, means shut the eyes in perplexity, trouble, disappointment or disgust.

negai, a vb., implore, beg, beseech.

negawamu, neg. of *negai*.

nenjite (*nen* in Chinese), p.part. *nenzuru* 念, prop. pray (to Buddha), in text, probably= resolutely, deliberately.

netaku, for *netamu*. See *netami*.

netami, a vb., be vexed about or with, dislike.

neya, sleep-chamber.

nezu, neg. *ne*, sleep.

nezumi. See *hi-nezumi*.

ni, p. position, in, by, on, etc., locative and instrumental. See also p. 70.

nichi (Ch.), day.

nige, run away.

nige-use, run out of sight.

nigiri, a vb., grasp.

nijiu (Ch.), twenty.

nikukarazu, not hateful or unpleasant.

nin (Ch.), man, person.

ninai, a vb., to bear as litter, etc.

ninawarete, pass. past part. of *ninai*, q.v.

nishi, west.

nishiki, a kind of patterned silk.

nite, sometimes p. part. of *naru* (*ni*), be, sometimes a postposition, meaning with, by, by means of, etc.

niwaka, sudden.

no, generic part. See p. 70.

no, moor.

nobori, ascend.

nochi, after (in time).

nokesama ni, backwards-falling, in supine manner.

nokori, be excepting, remain over.

nomare, quasi-pass. of *nomi*.

nomi, a vb., drink.

nonoshiri, a vb., in the text means 'shout' (also, shout abusively).

nori, be seated in or on.

nosesu (*noseshi*), cause to be placed or seated in or on.

notamai (*au*), say (honorific).

notamawase, caus. of *notamai*.

nozoki, a vb., peep through, take look at.

nugi-oku, take off-place, lay aside one's clothes, undress.

nuretaru, att. part. of *nure*, to be wet; an intrans. form of *nuri*.

nuri, a vb., besmear, wet, varnish.

nurigome, lit. plaster-enclosure, a fire-proof store-house.

nushi, lord, master, owner.

nusubito, thief (*nusumi*, *nusubi*, steal).

nyōnyō, groaningly, βαρυστενά-χων.

o, tail, in compos.

ō (*ohoku*, *ohoki*), great, big; *ō nusubito*, big thief.

ō (*ai*, *au*). See *ai*.

obosarezu, neg. pass. *oboshi*.

obosaru, *obosaruru*, quasi-pass. forms of *oboshi*, used as honorifics.

oboshi, a vb. (*obosu*), think-do, think, ponder.

oboshiki, seeming to be, like.

oboshi-nageki, think-grieve, be grieved about, weep with thinking over.

oboyezu, neg. *oboye*, think, perceive, remember.

ochi (*otsu*), fall from, drop.

ochi-inuru, past of *ochi*.

ochi-kakari, be ready to fall and strike upon or against, overwhelm.

ochinubeki, past potential or jussive.

odoro-odoroshiku, suspensive adjectival form, alarming(ly), agitated(ly).

ōgi. See *augi*.

ohoite. See *ōi*.

ohoku. See *ōku*.

oi, a vb., (*o-w-i*), grow.

ōi (*ohoi*), a vb., throw or put a covering over.

oi-harai, a vb., follow-drive, chase or drive or clear away.

oi-kaze, follow-wind, favourable wind.

oiraka ni, in a well-bred manner, composedly, properly. In the text, p. 48, the phrase should not be included in the quotation.

oitachi, compound a vb., grow up.

ōite (*ohoite*), p. part. a vb., *ōi*, q.v.

ōi-zukasa (*oho-i* 炊 大), chief kitchener.

ojinaki, awkward, vulgar; originally, perhaps, rude, ill-bred, as lacking respect for superiors.

ōkari(*u*)=*ōki-ari*, be big, many.

okashiku, pleasant, agreeable, excellent, nice (mod. ridiculous).

ōki (*ohoki*) *ni*, greatly.

oki, a vb., be on, lie, be in (position in space); often used transitively to mean put, place; *oki*, *i* vb., rise up; *oki-agari*, rise to one's feet.

oki mo agarazu=*mo oki-agarazu*.

okina, ancient, old man.

ōkisa, greatness, size.

okoshi, a vb., rouse; *omoi okoshi*, summon up resolution.

okose, e vb., send, despatch.

okoshi-tate, bring up (child).

ōku (ohoku), many, numerous; the attrib. *ōki=*big, vast.

okurishikeri, past form of *okuri.*

okuri, a vb., give, bestow.

omō. See *omoi.*

omobekere, emph. potent. past of *omoi.*

omoi, a vb. (*omo-y-w-i*), think, ponder; *mono wo o,* feel sad.

omoyeru (omohoyeru or *omohoyuru),* emphatic attrib. form of *omoi,* q.v.

omoi-ide, fall to thinking, etc.

omoi-nageki, think-lament, think over things up to lamenting.

omoi-sadamete, think-determine, consider and decide.

omoitsure, emph. past *omoi,* q.v.

omoi-wabi, to feel wretched with thinking.

omoi-yamu, cease thinking.

omoki, att. adj., heavy.

omomuki, a vb., go towards, go hence to (lit. face-present).

omonaki=omote naki, i.e. faceless=disappointed, mortified, put to shame.

omoshiroshi, agreeable, pleasant.

omote, face.

omoyeru (omoyuru), attrib. form of *omoi,* q.v.

omoyedomo, concessive of *omoi,* q.v.

on, honorific prefix, contraction of *ohon (ohomi,* grand).

ōna. See *onna.*

onaji, same.

oni, demon.

onna, for *omina,* woman, womanservant.

ono. See p. 61.

onoga. See p. 70.

onoko, male, son; also servants, retainers.

Onono Fusamori, name of retainer sent to Wōkei by the third suitor.

ori, be in (a place), remain at, be.

ori, a vb., break, break off.

orikite, descend-come, come down from.

orimono, woven fabric.

ori-ori, time-time, sometimes, time to time.

orite, ori, q.v.

oriteshikaba. See p. 85.

orokanaru, ignorant, simple, of low degree, boorish.

oroka-narazaru, neg. of *orokanaru,* q.v.

orosoka-naru, disrespectful, clownish.

oroshi, a vb., causat. of *ori,* descend, put on ground.

oru. See *ori.*

osanakereba, cond. of verbalised adj. *osanaku.*

osanaku, young, tender, inexperienced.

ōse (ohose), e vb., say (of superior), command, app. an honorific causative.

oshi, contracted for *oshishi,* concl. adject., pitiable.

oshi-kanashi, pitiably wretched.

oshiyesase, cause instruction to be given to . . .

ososhi (osoku, osoki), late, slow.

osoroshiku, suspens. adj., fearful, horrid.

8

osowaruru, be afraid of, be filled with dread.

oto, noise, rumour; *oto ni kiki*, be noised abroad; *oto mo sezu*, make no noise, i.e. be not heard of.

otoko, man.

Otomo, name of fourth suitor.

otori-masari, yield-excel, the worse or the better.

otoroye, lose power, strength, weaken.

otosamu, fut. *otoshi*, q.v.

otoshi, a vb., drop, let fall, deposit.

otosumeru, let drop, drop.

ouna. See *onna*.

owase (*owashi*), be in, at, be; an honorific causat. of a strengthened form of *i*; also charge, command.

owashimasenu(*zu*), neg. of *owase*, with addit. honorific *mashi*.

owashimashinu, past of *owase*, with addit. honorific *mashi*.

owashitari, past of *owase*.

owasu, conclusive of *owase*.

owasuramu, a future form of *owase*.

owasuru, attrib. *owase*.

oya, father.

ōyake, public.

ōzora, heavens, sky space.

ra, plural suffix, perhaps a fragment of *mura*.

rakai (Ch.), curtain or hangings, of what fabric is uncertain.

rei (Ch.), usual.

ri (Ch.), the Chinese *li* is meant in the text.

riyō (Ch.), a riyō (coin); also 料 device, trick, method.

roku (Ch.), pay, wage.

roku (Ch.), six.

rokuye (Ch.), the six regiments of palace guards.

ruri (Ch.), lapis lazuli, emerald, turquoise?

sa, contraction of *shika*, thus; also of *sari*, as in *saotodoshi*, q.v.

sabakari = *shika bakari*.

Sadaijin (Ch.), Left Great Minister.

sadaka, decided, settled.

sadamete, p. part. of *sadami*, decide, determine.

sadashite, *sadaka ni shite*. See *sadaka*.

sagashiri, so or *sore ga shiri*, his hinder parts.

sage, *e* vb., let down.

sage-oroshi, let down, set down.

saguru, *sage*.

saiwai (Ch.), fortunate.

sakagami, forelock.

sakashiki, adroit, able; -*kokoro*, strong-hearted, bold and strong.

saki, before, in front (time or place).

sama, way, method, appearance.

san (Ch.), three.

saotodoshi, year before year before last.

sara ni, moreover, quite.

sarasamu, fut. of *sarashi*, bleach by exposure.

sarazu, neg. *sari*, depart, go away from.

sarinamu = *sa-ari-namu*.

saritomo, *sa ari* or *shika ari to mo*, nevertheless.

saritote, albeit, however; *sa ari to iute* or *shite*.

saru, monkey; *saru toki*, hour of the monkey.

saru, *sa-aru*, thus-be, such sort of, such.

sasage, *e* vb., lift up, raise, offer as petition.

sasayaki, *a* vb., whisper, murmur.

sashi-iresasete, thrust - forward - cause-to-enter, i.e. take and put in.

sashi - megurashite, taking and causing to go or turn round.

sashi-ogi (*augi*), *a* vb. (?), lift up hands in grief, entreaty, etc.

sasuga ni, and so, of course; *shika-su-nagara*.

sate, well, well then, now; *shika shite*.

sawarazu, neg. of *a* vb. *sawari*, unhindered, in spite of; p. 46 *sawari*, also means to touch, strike against.

saye (*sahe*), even, also; with neg. not at all.

sayō (Ch.), thus, so.

sechi ni (Ch.), earnestly, intently.

seishi (Ch.), *sei* verbalised, reprove.

sekai (Ch.), world, this world.

seki-tome, *e* vb. (comp.), restrict, keep within bounds, etc.

semete, at least.

semu, fut. *shi* (*suru*), do.

sen (Ch.), a thousand.

sen. See *semu*.

sesasetamōbeki, honorific poten. caus. of *shi* (*suru*).

seyo, imperat. *shi* (*suru*), do.

sezu, neg. of *shi* (*suru*), do.

shaku (Ch.), Chinese foot (measure).

shi (*suru*), do; *-haberamu*, *-tamō*, *-ki* (past), *-ta* (past), *-te* (p. part.).

shi, a particle, an expletive emphasising preceding word.

shibashi, for a little time; used adjectivally (with *no*), adverbially (with *ni*).

shichi (Ch.), seven.

shige-yama, thickly over-grown shrubby hill.

shikaru, *shika aru*, be thus; *shikar edomo*, concessive form.

shiite, p.part. *shii*, *shiiru* (*i* vb.), oblige, compel, urge.

shikemu, a fut. part. form of *shi*, with aux. *ki*.

shikeru, an attrib. part. of *shi*, with aux. *ki*.

shiki, concl. past of *shi* (*suru*), do.

shiki (Ch.), colour, hue; *go shiki*, five colours (of rainbow).

shikite, *shiki*, spread, as a carpet, mat, etc.

shikomete, keep or put within something.

shimo, under, below, beneath.

shimo, hoar-frost; *-tsuki*, eleventh month.

shinaba, hypoth. part. *shinu* (*shi-ini*, do-go-away, i.e. finish with active life), die.

shini. See above.

shinobi, *a* vb. (*i* verb), avoid publicity; also endure, long for.

shirade, neg. p. part. *shiri*.

shirame, white-eye, eyes turned up so as to show the white (as in fainting).

shiranu, neg. *shiri*, know.

shirazu, neg. *shiri*.

shire ni shirete, an emphatic phrase = *shiretaru*, foolish, awkward, useless.

shiri, a vb., know, be aware of.

shirinu, past of *shiri*, q.v.

shiriseba, *shiri*, with condit. aux. *shi*, do.

shirite, p. part. *shiri*.

shirizokite, p. part. *shirizoki*, a vb., return, withdraw, retire.

shirogane, white metal, i.e. silver.

shiroku, suspensive adj., white.

shirushi, sign, token.

shisokuseshite, causing a light (*shisoku*, Ch.) to be brought.

shitagate, p. past *shitagai*, a vb., follow.

shitagawazu, neg. of *shitagai*. See *shitagate*.

shitakumi, resourceful, crafty, ἐολόμητις.

shitari, *shite ari*.

shitsurai, a vb., put to rights, prepare, build, construct, complete (as an interior), etc.

shiwasu, twelfth month.

shiwo, brine, salt-water.

shiyetari.

shizuka ni, tranquilly, composedly.

shōga (Ch.). See p. 47, vocal serenade, song.

shōji, *shōzuru*, *shō*, is Chinese 請 invite ; *shōji-iri*, being invited in, to enter.

shōshō, a military rank, major-general.

shōzoku (Ch.), raiment.

so ga = *sore ga*.

so, an imperat. final particle ; *na shitamai so*, do not, I beg, do so.

so, garment ; also *zo*.

soba-zura, side-face, slope (of a hill).

soko, bottom, also there.

sokora, thereabouts, there.

somete, p.part. *e* vb., *some*, dye.

somosomo, well then ! something like French ' or.'

somukaba, *somuki*, a vb. See *somukubeki*.

somukubeki, pot. of *somuki*, oppose.

sono, that, used adjectivally.

sora, strictly what intervenes between heaven and earth, air ; *sora mo naku*, distractedly.

soragoto, empty, false, counterfeit thing.

sōraikemu, fut. part. of *soro* (*samurai*), with auxil. *ki*.

sore, that.

sō-sesase, caus. of *sōsu*.

sōshi, Chinese 奏 verbalised by *su*, report to Mikado, superior, etc.

soshiri-ayeri, join in reproaching.

soyeru, quasi-pass. or intrans. form of *soi*, a vb., be united to, joined with, etc.

sōzoku (Ch.). See *shōzoku*.

su, nest ; *su wo kui*, build nest.

subekameru, a peculiar sort of double potential *su-beki-arame*, or perhaps there was at one time a future form of *beki*, *bekamu*.

suberi, a vb., slip.

sugata, form, shape.

sugi, *i* vb., pass by, excel, surpass; in comp. excess or completion.

sugi-wakare, be parted from and go away.

suguru, attrib. form of *sugi*.

sugushi, a vb. = *sugoshi*, pass, exceed, pass on (in time).

sugusugu to = *sugu to*, at once.

suji, *take hito suji*, one bamboo, lit. bamboo-one-stem. This ἅπαξ λεγόμενον is the only Japanese numerative found in the text.

suki, a vb., like, be fond of.

sukoshi, few, little; with *no* = adj., without *no*, adverb.

sukui, a vb., help, save.

sukunakarazu, sukunaku-arazu, not few, little, small.

sumitamawamu, sumi, a vb., dwell, with auxil. *tamai*.

sumomo, a sort of hard, sour plum, sloe, bullace.

sun (Ch.), inch (nearly).

sunawachi, then, so then, that is.

suredomo, concess. of *shi, suru*, do.

suri, rub.

suru, attrib. form of *shi*, q.v.

Suruga, a province of the main island.

susuro, suzuro, sozoro, suzuro-naru shini, sudden death or unforeseen death.

susuzukitaru, smoke-blackened.

sute, *e* vb. (*sutsuru*), abandon, cast away.

sutete, p. part. of *sute*.

suye, *e* vb., to place, find place for, lodge.

tabakari, a vb., deceive, impose upon one, beguile.

tabase, causat. of *tabe*, q.v.

tabe = *tamaye*.

tabi, journey, travel.

tabi = *tamai*, but with distincter sense of bestowing.

  -*okure*, bestow-give, deign to give.

  -*shikado*, contraction of *tabi* (*tamai*) *shi-ki-to-mo*.

tachi (*tatsu*), a vb., stand up, start.

  -*i*, be standing up.

  -*wakare*, take leave and start.

  -*noboru*, start-climb, set out to climb up, ascend.

  -*tsurare*, stand poised.

tachi, a plural suffix; *kimi-tachi*, lords.

tada, only, but, ordinary.

  -*bito*, common person, only a man, ordinary mortal.

  -*koto*, ordinary circumstance, or series of events.

tadare, be sore, red, inflamed; *me no tadare*, blear-eyed.

tadashi, a vb., arrange, put right; conjunction, but (at beginning of a phrase).

tadayoi, a vb., toss about; *tadayoheru*, be tossing about, i.e. looming over.

taga = *tarega*, whose? of whom?

tagai, a vb. (*taga-w-y-i*), not correspond to, conform to, fit, etc.; *tagamawashikaba*, hyp. past form.

tagoshi, litter borne by men.

tagui-naku, incomparable.

taidai-shiku (Ch.), unobservant of, neglectful.

taimen (Ch.), face to face, meet, have interview with ; *-shi tamaye*, pray receive.

taishite (Ch.), 帶, be girdled with, be slung with.

Taka no Okuni, prop. name.

takaki, attrib. adj., high, lofty.

takara, treasure.

take, bamboo.

take, stature.

takeki, bold.

Taketori, Bamboo-hewer.

takumi, craftsman, artist, skill, resource.

tama, jewel.

tamai, is sometimes used (p. 58, l. 24) as a principal verb, to bestow : more commonly as an auxil. honorific merely.

tamainu, past of *tamai*.

tamaine, past emph. of *tamai*.

tamaiten, *tamaitemu*, perhaps a past future, with auxiliary *tsuru*.

tamawamu, fut. *tamai*.

tamawarite, *tamai-ari*, quasi-pass. of *tamai*.

tamawasen, fut. caus. of *tamai*.

tamaye, emphatic of *tamai*, used as imperative.

tamayeri, *tamai-ye(u)-ari*, or *tamai-ari*.

tamasaka ni, occasionally.

tamashii, precious-breath, soul, 'anima.'

tamazakaru. See p. 16.

tamoto, sleeve.

tanomi, a vb., request, request aid, trust to ; *tanomi wo kake*, present request or petition, maintain suit.

tanome, an intrans. form of *tanomi*.

tanomoshigari, *tanomoshi-ge-ari*. See *tanomoshigenaki*.

tanomoshigenaki, helpless, aidless, feeble, giving no assistance.

taorade, neg. part. *taori*, hand-break, break off.

tashika, certain, sure, firm.

tasuke, e vb., help, aid.

tatakō (*au*), a vb., *tatakai*, fight with.

tatazumi, a vb., stand still in a place.

tate, e vb. (a sort of quasi-pass. of *tachi*, stand up, having a transitive force).

tatematsuru, a humilific auxiliary.

tatōbeki, attrib. potential auxil. form of.

tawayasuku, app. an old or emphatic form of *tayasuku*, easy.

taye, come to end, fail, cease, also endure, suffer, bear ; *taye-iri*, expire, die.

tayegata (*tayegatashi*), hard to endure, insupportable. See p. 24 n.

tayuru, attrib. *taye*.

te, hand ; *te wo wakachite*, distributing in bands or companies.

Temujiku, India (*Tenjiku*).

tera, Buddhist temple.

terashi, caus. *teri*, a vb., shine.

teri-kagayaku, shine-dazzle, shine and sparkle, glitter, etc.

teri-hatataku (*ha-tataki*, clap-wings), shine-clap-thunder, lightning and thunder.

to. See p. 71.

to (*soto*), *to ni sarasamu*, will expose outside.

tō (*toi*), a vb., ask, request, inquire.

tō (*toku*), fast, swift.

tobi, a vb., fly.

tobikarasu, a kind of crow.

toburai, a vb., make visit of condolence or ceremony.

Tōchi, place-name.

todome, e vb., stop, hinder, restrain.

todomesase, causat. (aux.) of *todome*.

togenaki, successless, luckless, bootless, etc.

toi, a vb. (*to-w-y-i*), ask, inquire.

toi-sawagi, a vb., ask and be agitated, make fervent inquiry of.

to-kaku, this-that, thus and thus, etc.; -*mōsu*=hesitate, shilly-shally.

toki, time; *toki ni*, when (also *toki*).

tokoro, place; modern quasi-relative use not exemplified in text.

toku. See *tō*.

tokuchi, door-entrance, doorway.

tōkute (*tohoku shite*); *tohoku*= susp. adj., distant, far.

tomare (*to mo are*). See *to kaku*.

tomari, a vb. (*tome-ari*), stop, stay, rest.

tono, lord, master; originally mansion or palace.

toneri, palace-attendant.

tōrai=*toburai*, q.v.

tōraji, neg. fut. *tōri*, a vb., pass through or by.

torase, caus. of *tori*, a vb., seize, take.

toraye, e vb., = *tori*, strengthened in sound as in meaning.

toreru, quasi-pass. *tori*.

toreyede, *tori*, a vb., take, neg. p. part., quasi-pass.

toridashi or *tori-idashi*.

torisutesase, cause to take and throw away (destroy).

toritemu, a fut. form of *tori*.

toru. See *tori*.

tose. See *toshi*.

toshi, year.

tote, for *to iite* or *to shite*.

tōtoshi, *tōtoku* (*tattoshi*), concl. adj., honourable, noble.

towase. See *towasuru*.

towasuru, attrib. caus. of *toi*, ask, etc.

toyaba, hypoth. of *toi*.

tsu, a generic particle=*no*, also past suffix. See p. 70.

tsubakarame, swallow (*tsubame*).

tsubo, jar, bowl.

tsubure, e vb., be broken, spoilt, destroyed.

tsuchi, soil, earth.

tsuge, e vb., tell, communicate to.

tsugi, a vb., *inochi wo tsugu*, keep up life.

tsui-hi-ji(*tsuki-hi-ji*). There seems to be some doubt whether this means platform of beaten earth for the house to stand on, or an earthen parapet or terrace.

tsui ni, at last, in the end.

tsukai, a vb. (*tsukau-ô*), employ, use, have service of.

tsukamatsuri, a vb., humilific auxil. verb ; also, do, etc.

tsukami-tsubushi, a vb. (comp.), seize and throw over or down.

tsukawaruru, quasi-pass. of *tsukai*.

tsukasa, chief of an order of functionaries.

tsukawashi (*tsukawasu*, *tsukawashishi*), a vb., lit. cause to send (i.e. send), a more honorific form than *tsukai*, send.

tsuke, e verb, stick, fix, hang on to, fasten to; *hito wo tsuke*, fix upon a person.

tsukesasu (*tsuke-sashi*), *sashi*, has sense of reaching or putting forward from one.

tsukômatsuramu, fut. of a form of *tsukamatsuri*, q.v., having more distinctly the meaning 'serve.'

tsuki, moon, month.

tsuki, a vb., consume, use up, come to end of.

tsuki, a vb., *awohedo wo tsuki*, hawk up green vomit.

tsukinaki, may mean unattainable or unbearable.

tsuku no ana goto ni, where each pillar pierced (or supported) the roof.

tsukumodokoro, workshop. See p. 85.

tsukuri-hana, artificial flower.

tsukurase, causat. of *tsukuri*, a vb., make, manufacture; *tsumi wo tsukari*, commit sin.

tsukushi, a vb., exhaust.

Tsukushi, old name of north-western portion of Kiushiu.

tsukushi-hate, exhausted.

tsume, nail, *unguis*.

tsumi, sin, fault.

tsuna, rope, cord.

tsune, ordinary, common ; *tsune ni*, always, commonly.

tsurane, e vb., place in series, connect.

tsurazuye (*tsura-suye*, face-rest), the position of resting the face or chin on the hand.

tsurare-noborite, accompanied-climb, ascend in company with.

tsuri-agesase, suspend-raise, draw up by a line or rope.

tsuru, past auxiliary ; *aritsuru*, etc.

tsutsu, hollow stem ; also a past suffix. See p. 79.

tsuyoku, suspensive adj., strong.

tsuyu, dew, dewdrop; *tsuyu mo mono sora ni kakeraba*, should even so much as a drop of dew shower down through the air.

ube, adj. root, good, excellent, right.

uchi, within, in.

uchi, subst. house (more modern).

uchi, a verb (*utsu*), strike, in comp. gives emphasis, sense of suddenness or beginning.

uchi-age, lift up (the rue-beer or spirit-bowl), hence, drink (at feast).

uchi-ide, go, come-forth.

uchi-irete, put in.

uchi-kake, be on point of toppling over into (of the waves, p. 42), overhang, be imminent over, strike at, etc.

uchi-kise, put-on (transitive).

uchi-kubete, p.part. cast in.

Uchimaro, family-name of artisans who make the Bloom branch.

Uchimaro-ra, the Uchimaros, the U. family.

uchi-nageki, lament aloud, fall to lamenting, etc.

uchi-sugi, pass away, pass by (of time).

udomuguye (*udonge*). See p. 11.

ugokarenu, neg. quasi-pass. *ugoki*, move.

ugokashi, causat. *ugoki*, move.

ukabi (*ukabu*), a vb., swim, float.

ukagai, a vb., inquire, ask, investigate.

ukagawasemu, caus. of *ukagai*.

uketamawarazaramu (*uke-tamai-arazu-aramu*), neg. fut. *uke-tamawari*, receive, hear, obey.

uketsu, past of *uke*, e vb., receive.

uku, suspensive adj., sadly ; *mono uku omohoyete*, sadly pondering over things, i.e. pining.

umase, cause to bear; *umi*, a vb., bear, give birth to.

umashiki, att. adj., pleasant, sweet, nice.

umeru (*ume*), e vb., intrans. of *umi*, be born, get born.

umi, a vb., give birth to. Substantive, sea.

umu, a vb. See *umi*.

unazuki, a vb., nod assent.

unjite (Ch. *un-zuru*), verbalised Chinese, be wearied out, dejected.

ura, coast, tract of coast.

uramaji, fut. form of *urami*, q.v.

urami, a vb., be vexed at.

urawashiku. See *uruwashiku*.

ureshiku, suspensive adj., charming, delightful.

ureyeseshi, miserable, wretched.

uruwashiku, lovely.

use, e vb., disappear, fade away.

uso, *usofuki*, or *usowofuki*, whistle with mouth, perhaps from similarity to piping of bulfinches (*uso*).

usuru. See *use*.

uta, song, poem.

utagai, a vb., doubt, hesitate.

utai, a vb., sing, chant, compose song or poem.

utate-aru, ill-fated, sorrowful.

utena, outside balcony or gallery, or building having such.

utsukushiute, a verbal form of adj. *utsukushi(k)u*, beautiful, being beautiful.

utsushi, a vb., fall prone.

uye, above, over, on.

wa, isolative part. See p. 69.

wabi, i vb., supplicate, also be regretful, tired of, etc.

wabi-sase, causat. of *wabi*.

wabishiku, miserable.

wabishikime, miserable state of things.

waga, mine, his, some one's.

waga-mi, myself, etc.

wakachi, a vb. (*wakatsu*, *waka-chite*), distribute, allot.

waketsutsu (wake), *e* vb., divide, allot, distribute.

warawa, child.

ware, I, sometimes oneself; a pronoun of all persons.

warokarishi, att. part. of *waroku (waruku)*, with aux. *aru*, was bad, evil.

wasurare, quasi-pass. of *wasure*.

wasure, forget, *e* vb.

wata, cotton.

watari, *a* vb., cross over, pass along, go through.

waza, job, business.

wazuka, few, little, scant, slight.

wazurawashiku, painfully miserable.

wo, p.position to object of verb. See p. 70.

wo, interjectional particle; *tadashi . . . tama yuki-torashi wo, iwanya!* But, O, how to get hold of the jewel!

Wōkei, name of merchant who procured the Fur Robe.

ya, house; also interrogative and dubitative particle. See p. 72.

yadosu, *a* vb. (*yadoshi*), lodge, contain.

yagate, straightway.

yakamu, fut. of *a* vb. *yaki*, burn.

yake(te), intrans. form *yaki*, burn.

yakezuba, cond. neg. *yake*.

yakite, p.part. See *yakamu*.

yama, hill, mountain, uncultivated ground.

yamai, illness.

Yamato, name of a province of the main island.

yamemu, fut. *e* vb. *yame*, trans. of *yami*.

yami, *a* vb., cease; also be ill.

yami-fuseri, lie or throw oneself prostrate as if suddenly sick.

yamu, *yami*.

yamubeku, *yami*.

yaredomo, concessive of *yari*.

yarite, p.part. *yari*; on p. 57 it has almost sense of *quoad* (comp. English use of 'given.')

yari, *a* vb., give, bestow.

yasashi, concl. adj., easy, soft, gentle.

yashinau, *a* vb.(*yashinai*), cherish, bring up, nourish.

yashinawasu, causative of *yashinai*.

yasuki, att. adj., easy, peaceful ; p. 46, *yasuki i mo nezu=yasuku mo nezu.*

yasushi, concl. of *yasuki*.

yatsu, fellow, creature.

yatsubara, fellows, in a contemptuous sense.

yatsure, making a mean show, be starved in appearance, etc.

ye, p.position, to, towards.

ye, picture, drawing.

ye, *e* vb., obtain, procure; often used as an auxiliary giving potential sense ; *ye-mitsuke-tatematsurazu narinu* ; *ye-torase-tama-waji.*

yeda, branch.

ye-gata, difficult, impossible of procurement (conclus. *yega-tashi*).

yeitaru, attrib. part. *yei* or *yoi*, be drunk, intoxicated.

yemi-sakaye, break out into smile.

yemitsuketatematsurazu, (they) were unable to get sight of (him).

ye-oki-agari-tamawade, (his Highness) could not get up on his feet.

yerabi, a vb., choose, select.

yesemezu, without pressing or constraining.

yeshi, past of *ye*(*uru*), get, obtain.

yeshiinu, potent. of *shii,* q.v.

yeshirade, neg. potent. of *shiri,* q.v.

yetaru, past attrib. of (*ye, e, u, uru*), get, obtain.

yetatakawamu, fut.potent.*tatakai,* fight with.

yeteshi. See p. 82.

yo, excess; *sen yo mich,* a thousand days and more.

yo, I.

yo, night.

yo, age; *sæculum,* world.

yō, manner, purport.

yobai, intensitive form of *yobi,* call, seek out one's mistress, especially at night.

yobi, a vb., call, summon.

yobi-ide, go out and call.

yobi-suye, call-place, invite within.

yobi-tori, call-take.

*yobi-tsudoye,*call-gather-together, invite and assemble.

yogoto, prayer, invocation, charm, blessing.

yōji (Ch.), use, usage, service.

yokaru, yoku-aru, be good, right, etc.

yokashi=yoshi, good, right.

yoki, att. adj., good, right, etc.

yoku, suspensive adj. See *yoki.*

yomeru, intrans. of *yomi.*

yomi, a vb., read, recite, compose (verses).

yomi-kuwaye, compose and add to, compose additional (verses).

yonde=yomite. See *yomi;* also *yobite.*

yori, a vb., stop in passing by, approach; p. position, from, than.

yorikobi, a vb., be glad, joyful.

yori-kumajiki, neg. future of *yori-kuru,* come nigh, come up to, approach.

yori-mōde, approach. See *mōde.*

yorozu, ten thousand; *-no,* countless.

yoru. See *yori.*

yoru, night, night-time.

yo-sari, night-depart, i.e. dawn.

yosetari, concl. past; *yose,* caus. of *yori.*

yoshi. See *yoki.*

yoshi-nakari=yoshi·naki-ari, app. an irr. form for *yoku-naki.*

yosohoi, a vb., dress, adorn.

yowaku, suspensive adj., weak, feeble, ill.

yōyō (*yaya* or *yōyaku*), finally, at last.

yū, evening.

yuami, warm baths.

yui-agete, bind up (hair), tie (to a rope) and raise up, draw up.

yukashi, concl. adj., desirable, excellent.

yukamahoshiki (*yukamu-hoshiki*), desirous to go.

yuki-hate, kokoro yuki-hatete, p. 50, probably means 'her heart came to the end of (its suspense).' Perhaps *hate* ought to read *hare*, clear up, become free from clouds, annoyances, etc.

yuki-torashi, go cause-to-take, cause to obtain, acquire.

yuku-suye, path or track; also future, i.e. path or track henceforth.

yumi, bow (the weapon).

yumiya, bow and arrow, warrior.

yumizu, warm water.

yurusaji, neg. of *yurushi* (*yuru-su*), permit, allow.

yutaka, abundance, affluence, opulence.

yuyami, evening-darkness, nights moonless and dark.

zeni, a fully-naturalised Chinese word (Ch. *ts'ien*), a cash; equivalent to present *sen*. Compare *fumi* (文).

zo, an emphatic particle. See p. 72; see also *so*.

ADDENDA.

P. 84. *urami mo uramaji;* a better illustration is the common biblical form of phrase, *niksôph niksaphta,* נִכְסֹף נִכְסַפְתָּ.

P. 88. *i(ite) ;* this is not, probably, an *o* verb.

The author must express his obligations to his colleague, Mr. T. Le Marchant Douse, for some valuable suggestions in relation to the philology of the foregoing pages.

STEPHEN AUSTIN AND SONS, PRINTERS, HERTFORD.

www.ingramcontent.com/pod-product-compliance
Lightning Source LLC
Chambersburg PA
CBHW020756020726
47495CB00008B/2458